CHINA SAILOR

CHINA SAILOR

Charles Giezentanner

Cover design by Chuck Giezentanner

iUniverse, Inc.
Bloomington

China Sailor

iUniverse books may be ordered through booksellers or by contacting:

iUniverse
1663 Liberty Drive
Bloomington, IN 47403
www.iuniverse.com
1-800-Authors (1-800-288-4677)

ISBN: 978-1-4759-3203-4 (sc)
ISBN: 978-1-4759-3205-8 (hc)
ISBN: 978-1-4759-3204-1 (ebk)

Library of Congress Control Number: 2012910102

Printed in the United States of America

iUniverse rev. date: 06/05/2012

Leslie Charles

The USS *Guam*

CHAPTER 1

AMERICA

Leslie Charles is an eighteen-year-old young man from Madison County, North Carolina. Leslie had a year of college at Mars Hill College. Mars Hill is a small college town also in Madison County, North Carolina.

It is 1938, right in the middle of the Great Depression. Young Leslie comes from a large family consisting of his mother and father, three brothers, and two sisters. Leslie is the oldest of the children. Leslie is six feet tall, slim, muscular, and has dark hair and eyes. He can play the violin, guitar, and other stringed instruments very well. Leslie is smart. He likes to dream, and he loves running and fishing, but he does not like getting dirty. Leslie has never had a professional haircut; his hair looks like an upside-down bowl. One of Leslie's brothers is Albert, who is thirteen and smart and also plays all stringed instruments. He is going to look kind of like Leslie when he is the same age, and so will the other boys—John Henry, twelve; Frank, eleven; and Little Herbert (pronounced "a bear"), four. Leslie has two beautiful sisters: Ava, nine, and Sonja, eight. Leslie's father is named Otto and is now close to forty. Otto came to America when his father, Herbert (pronounced "a bear") Charles, brought him and his two brothers and sister to America looking for a good life for his family. Otto was eleven and played the violin;

John, six, violin; Etta, five, violin; and Franz, two. He did not want to play anything, and he was already as tall as John and Etta.

It was 1907 when the Charles family arrived at Ellis Island from Geneva, Switzerland. Mrs. Charles, the wife of Herbert (pronounced "a bear") and the mother of the Charles children, died on the voyage over the Atlantic. The ship was so overcrowded and had little in the way of sanitation that a couple of hundred people died on the voyage.

At this time in America, anti-Semitism was growing. Ellis Island was being run by the Irish. The Irish police, Irish clerks, and Irish immigration officers had decided that New York had too many non-English-speaking Jews, so they put the new Jews on railcars and shipped them south. When the trains crossed the Mason-Dixon Line, the conductors started putting families off. The Charles family was put off the train in Johnson City, Tennessee. Johnson City did not have any Jews and did not really want any.

No one in the family could speak English, so they could not find work. Herbert, a master musician in Europe, finally had to use sign language to find food and shelter for his family, and he was able to pick up day labor work, like digging up septic systems, cleaning barns, repairing all kinds of structures, and picking up and burying roadkill. Herbert trapped, and he and Otto fished while the other children forged for nuts and berries and gathered firewood and water. In the evenings, Herbert held music lessons for his children; they each practiced the violin and the guitar, and he taught them to read music and to read and write German. Each person would say an English word, and the rest would practice it. Otto learned the most words; he had a knack for sounds and words. Otto was also the best at the violin. Otto was bigger and stronger than the rest.

The family spent their first year in America living in a corncrib, a large lean-to that was dry. Otto got day labor jobs at the rail yard, the saw mill, and the cattle yard. He hung around the Western Union office at the rail yard when he did not work; he was fascinated by the telegraph and the new teletype machines. The employees were surprised at how fast Otto had learned to operate both machines. They all said that he had an ear for sounds.

Mr. Herbert Charles finally got a job working for the old spinster lady in the next town over called Jonesboro, in Tennessee. A really nice place. Her name was Stella George. Stella had been the youngest of three children. Stella's parents had been a Free Church minister and his wife a schoolteacher. Both had passed away within a year of each other. Stella had stayed with her parents to take care of them in their later years. Stella's brother and sister had married and moved to Johnson City many years ago.

Stella had inherited the family farm that her folks had owned. It was fifteen acres of rocks, although it had two creeks full of fish that ran through it. Stella lived in a four-room sharecropper's house on the property. There was a well house, a root cellar, a small barn with a carriage shop, and an outhouse. Stella made her money by sewing and selling aprons, clothes, pen bags, and sun bonnets. Stella made and sold jellies and jams (apple, blackberry, gooseberry, and cherry). She kept bees and sold honey. Stella was well-off by mountain standards. She worked hard but knew she was forty and all alone. Herbert and his children moved into Stella's carriage shop, which was part of the barn. It had a real door and two real windows. Herbert spent the next two years, during his spare time, putting in a floor, porches, and roofs over the porches. Herbert made three rooms out of the place and added a wood stove for central heat. Things were looking up for the family.

Herbert ("a bear") was now thirty-seven years old. He began to sneak up to Stella's little house for some companionship. Stella is now forty-one and lonely. Herbert was the educated, well-spoken gentleman she had been waiting for her whole life. It's now the second Christmas at the farm for the family, and the Charles family decided to sing Christmas carols for Ms. Stella George. Herbert and Otto played the violins, Etta played the guitar, John played a kind of bass he had made, and Franz sang. Stella had cookies and milk for them. That night, the Charles family stayed with Ms. Stella George for a family Christmas. A few weeks later, Stella and Herbert married. Stella got Herbert the job of a janitor at her church, and he played the piano for the church choir. The kids also played and sang for the choir. Herbert started giving piano and violin lessons to the children of Jonesboro. Herbert and Stella believed in education and hard work, so the children started public schools for the first time and loved it, except for Franz. Franz was a bully at school. He had been abused by all the neighborhood children for many years, which made him grow into a bully himself, but all the girls loved him. His grades weren't very good either. Stella and Hebert thought that maybe Franz was a little brain damaged or just slow.

In the evenings, after all the chores and homework and supper were finished, Herbert and Stella held their own school. Stella taught each child how to cook, sew, eat, dress, talk, and walk like upper-class children. Herbert taught music and math.

Herbert Charles got a job in Mars Hill, North Carolina, as a stringed instrument instructor and repairman at the Baptist College of Mars Hill. Stella got a job as a breakfast cook at the Woman's Hill, a women's dorm. Stella, Herbert, and the children moved into the faculty housing on campus in 1913. It was a nice big house with indoor plumbing. John Charles could start his college career at Mars Hill College for free.

CHAPTER 2

//

OTTO CHARLES

At sixteen, Otto was offered and took a job at the railroad as a telegraph and teletype operator. He also learned how to install and operate these machines. Otto went to public school for another year but then took a full-time job at the railroad. He continued his lessons at home. Otto began to travel to eastern Tennessee and western North Carolina, helping to set up the teletype offices and training the operators. He loved his job, he liked the mountains, and he liked having some money in his pocket. Otto started working and living in Sweetwater, Tennessee, He was working when he met a young lady who was only fifteen. Her name was Brigitta Miesenhammer; she was five foot eleven, slender, and a German Jew. She was a waitress at the local café. She served the workers and tourists at the Craighead Caverns.

These caverns were used by Cherokee Indians as a meeting place and a high holy place. During the Civil War, the Confederates used them to mine saltpeter (used for making gun powder). The caverns have some of the largest crystal clusters called anhydrites, stalactites, stalagmites, and a very large waterfall. It has America's largest underground lake.

Brigitte came from an upper-class family. They owned a shoe store, a small grocery store, a barber shop, and a horse-trading business. The Miesenhammers had a car and a large home. Brigitte was self-taught; she studied bookkeeping, law, and business. Brigitte did not like cooking or cleaning or any of the things traditional women did; she liked business. Brigitta spoke English, German, and Yiddish. Brigitta was fifteen and Otto was twenty when the couple married. Brigitta was tall and handsome, not beautiful but nice looking. Otto was five foot eight and muscular and also very nice looking. They moved in with Brigitte's family. Otto was usually gone for five days and four nights a week, so he only had to stay with the Miesenhammers on weekends. He did not mind. His in-laws seemed to really like him. Otto turned his check over to Brigitta and she would give him a weekly allowance. Brigitte told Otto that she would keep the money and take care of the bills for him. She was able to save money each week after their bills were paid.

Otto and Brigitte were transferred to Asheville, North Carolina, with the railroad in the telegraph and teletype office. Otto was now the assistant foreman in the office. Otto and Brigitta bought a small home on Hazzard Street in downtown Asheville. Brigitta had made and saved enough money to buy herself a 1911 Buick truck with a steel top. They had their first child in 1919. It was a boy, and they named him Leslie, after Brigitte's grandfather. Brigitte's first job in Asheville was selling tombstones. She liked this job. She could carry her samples in the back of the truck and Leslie in the front. Brigitta was very good at selling tombstones. She would laugh and say, "I have sold more granite stones for Confederate generals to sleep under at Riverside Cemetery than it took to build the Vance Monument."

The Vance Monument was built in the center of Asheville to honor the Civil War governor of North Carolina, Zebulon B. Vance. Vance was a champion for human rights, constitutional rights for individual rights. He forced the Confederate Congress to add the writ of habeas corpus to the Confederate Constitution, and he championed Jewish rights.

Brigitte was very good at having families replace the small old grave markers with nice large new granite ones. It was the American dream for them. After four years, Brigitta starting having more children. She and Otto ended up with seven in all. They had Leslie, Albert, John Henry, Frank, Ava, Sonja, and Little Herbert ("a bear"). Brigitta and Otto also believed in teaching their children the meaning of good hard work. The family moved into a new home on Cumberland in the Montford area. It was very large. It had eight bedrooms and three and a half baths—five bedrooms on the second floor with a bath, three bedrooms and a bath on the third floor, and a half bath on the first floor with a formal setting room, a formal dining room, a kitchen, a breakfast room, an office, and a music room. The basement had a bath, a canning room, a laundry room, two storage rooms, and an indoor playing room. The family had a piano, violins, a bass, and two new radios. Otto had bought himself a Ford motor car. Brigitta bought herself a new car also. It was a 1928 Chrysler Imperial. Otto had it kind of tough. He had to cook and help clean the house. Brigitta did neither of these chores. The family decided they had to hire a maid who could cook. They hired a colored lady with razor-cut scars on her face called Ruth. Ruth lived in the basement. Brigitta bought a 1927 Maytag electric clothes washer. Boy, were they rich.

In 1929, during the Great Depression, the whole country went broke, and so did the Charles family. The company Brigitta worked for closed, and the railroad laid men off. Otto had to work his shift and a half shift; it added up to seventy hours a week and included an all-nighter once a week. Brigitta told Ruth she would have to go,

Ruth begged, "Miss Charles, let me stay. I'll work for free. I have nowhere to go." Brigitta agreed that Ruth could stay. As the weeks went by, the times looked bleaker. The country was in really bad shape. By now 20 percent of the workforce had been laid off. Months went by, and Brigitta had to sell her beloved truck. Otto had to park his car and take the electric trolley to work and back. The car costs too much money to operate. Ruth's sister Lara Ann showed up at the Charles's home looking for work. She told Ruth and Mrs. Charles that the laundry at the hotel she worked for had closed down, and she had no place to go.

7

This gave Brigitta an idea. "Ruth," she said, "your sister may stay in your room tonight, and then I'll make a decision what to do with her." The next morning, Brigitta drove to the ten-room hotel in downtown Asheville where Lara Ann had worked. She asked the owner what he was going to do about his laundry (the hotel towels, sheets, pillowcases, and his family laundry).

"I'll have to send them to one of the local laundries," he replied.

"What do they charge you for all the laundry?" He gave her the price list the laundry had given him. Across it, it also said, "NO MIXING OF WHITES." Brigitta laughed and said, "Everybody knows you do not mix your colors. They will fade on each other."

The hotel owner laughed and said, "That is not what that means. It means no colored person's clothes will be washed with white people's clothes."

"Oh," she replied. Brigitta thought to herself, *I'll bet that most laundry workers are colored, and I'll guarantee they wash their clothes with the whites.* Brigitta said she would do all the laundry for the hotel and his family and the guests and take one penny off of each item listed on the price sheet, and she would keep the clothes separated, but she said, "I don't know of any reason why I would do any colored people's clothes." The hotel manager/owner said it was a deal. He had two very large bags of laundry ready to go. He had to load them in the Imperial, and Brigitta drove off with them. Brigitta went into the basement and told Lara Ann and Ruth that Lara Ann could also stay, but she had to do the laundry and there was no money to pay her either, only room and board. The two ladies agreed; they had no other place to go. The next day Brigitta went to a larger hotel in Asheville, about thirty rooms, and offered the same laundry deal for them. They had closed down their laundry weeks before.

The manager asked, "Do you do colored laundry also?"

Brigitta had to think. *Why does he want to know that?* She then saw a cleaning lady in a white and gray starched uniform cleaning the floors. "Yes, I do, but I don't mix, if you know what I mean," was her reply. He smiled and said, "I'll be happy to do business with you. Besides the regular laundry she would have to do, she also had to starch and iron two maids' and an elevator operator's uniforms. Things may be looking up a little bit for the Charles family. Brigitta made a deal with the hotel owner to buy his old commercial Maytag and his folding tables, irons, and pressing machine.

Ruth asked when they were to do the colored clothes—before or after the sheets? Brigitta said do them all together; she was not going to waste time or supplies to do two jobs when one would be fine. Just don't tell anybody.

Brigitta and Otto were from European Jews; they had seen what prejudice is in Tennessee. They did not judge people by their color or religion but by their education and what was in their hearts. They never tried to force their ideas on anyone, nor did they want anyone to try to force ideals on them.

CHAPTER 3

LESLIE CHARLES

L eslie Charles, oldest child of Otto and Brigitta, got a job after school working for the water department in Asheville. He would fill in the holes the department made putting in a water line in a new section of West Asheville. He was paid his family's water bill and two bits a day (twenty-five cents). With the amount of water his family was using, it was a bargain. Leslie was sixteen and strong and he liked the work. Being Caucasian and sixteen made Leslie one of four foremen on one of the digging crews. The city served the digging crews very weak soup and biscuits for lunch. Leslie had Ruth from his mom's house always pack him a lunch. Leslie noticed that a couple of colored men on the digging crews did a faster, cleaner job on the digs, which meant that their foreman would not have to stay over and help fix what they had messed up. Leslie started having Ruth pack three extra sandwiches with his lunch; he would give them to the three best diggers and have them on his crew. It worked. These men appreciated the sandwiches and worked hard and neat for Leslie. He really liked being the boss and figuring out how to make his crew better.

He worked after school and the summer until he graduated in 1936 and went to Mars Hill College the next year. He studied math and music. Before going into his second year at Mars Hill, he heard that the navy yard in Norfolk was hiring college students to work for college monies. Leslie signed up and was sent to Norfolk. Leslie needed the money, and he wanted the new adventure and maybe a place for him to learn about women. Leslie had a little trouble with the girls at Mars Hill; he seemed too shy to even talk to them.

Leslie had a good mind and body, and with his math background, they assigned him to learn welding. At the same time Leslie was moving to Norfolk, his uncle Franz was moving to Asheville.

CHAPTER 4

FRANZ CHARLES

He had to move from Mars Hill, from Madison County to anywhere, just out of the county. The sheriff of Madison County and the chief of police of Mars Hill and the concerned citizens of Madison County said that Franz was not ever welcome to come back. Franz had spent two years in the army in the big war. He spent the last six months of his army life in the brig. He had tried to cut an X on the forehead of a British sailor. Franz was stationed outside of New Orleans, at a very basic German school. His job was to teach the troops basic street signs and basic commands like "halt," "stop," "throw down your weapons," "who's in charge," "do you need help," "will you surrender," and many other German words. Franz, being born in Europe and speaking German, the army was not sure which army he would be loyal to. So instead of fighting in the trenches, Franz would fight in the bars and bordellos. He gambled and drank most of his time away in the army. Franz made private first class three different times but was busted back to private each time. Franz did not care; he made plenty of money gambling and hustling in the barracks. Many months after the war ended, Franz was released from the brig. He stayed in New Orleans. He became a professional hustler, gambler, collector, and he tried private boxing. He liked to beat up people, but some of these boxers had boxed professionally, and Franz had trouble besting them. He even got hurt a few times, so he decided to stick with what he did best—gamble, hustle, run the women, and collect bad debts for the local gamblers. Franz traveled the Southern cities, hustling. He met a colored man with red hair called Isaiah Green in Cuba. He was also a hustler and a gambler. Isaiah was almost as tall as Franz. Franz was six feet tall, but Isaiah was a very thin man. He also had about ten years on Franz. He and Isaiah traveled and worked together for many years.

Franz found out that Isaiah was from Asheville, where Franz's big brother Otto and his family lived. In 1937 Isaiah called his mother on her birthday. She had troubling news for him, and he had to come home. Franz said, "I'll go with you, and I need to see my family. I've not seen them in thirteen to fourteen years." Isaiah had a Chrysler, so the men drove from Miami to Tampa, Florida, to Asheville, North Carolina. They drove straight through without stopping except for gas, food, and bathroom breaks. They drove to Eagle Street in downtown Asheville, where Isaiah Green's family lived. Franz took a cab to the train depot where his older brother and one of the very few people he ever listened to worked. He felt that he really wanted to see his brother. He told his brother he was in for business and would stay with him a few days. He wanted to get to Mars Hill to see his dad and the rest of his family. He told Otto that he had driven for fifteen hours and he needed to sack out. Otto gave him a choice of a large room in the basement with a bath to share or the spare bedroom on the second floor, but he would have to share the bath with him and Brigitta and some of the kids. Franz took the basement. Franz called Isaiah and told him where he was and asked what was going on in his family. Neither man had told each other of their families.

Isaiah told Franz that his mother was known as Blind Janie, that she was a large blind colored woman who a lot of people on Eagle Street were in fear of. She liked to cut people with a straight razor if you crossed her. She ran numbers and Sunday alcohol sales.

Buncombe County was a county where no mixed drink sales—just beer and unfortified wine were allowed (unfortified wine was wine under 13 percent alcohol)—and no alcohol on Sundays. Blind Janie also ran an employment company; most of the maids in Asheville had to pay Janie a dime for each week they worked for white families.

Her brother was called Daddy Rabbit. He ran the gambling in colored neighborhoods. He ran a club called Daddy Rabbit's. It was one of those clubs where if you went into the club and were not armed, they would give you a gun—not really, but it was a rough club. Daddy Rabbit was dying, and the family needed a new Daddy Rabbit. Blind Janie wanted to be Daddy Rabbit but was blind and knew she could not handle it. So Isaiah Green was chosen by the family to be the new head of the family. Isaiah would now be the fourth Daddy Rabbit.

Leslie and Franz looked like twins. Both were six foot tall, well built, with black hair and black eyes, and very nice looking. Leslie could play the violin, but Franz could not even hum. Franz would rather steal the violin and pawn it.

The local pawn dealers in Madison County knew if Franz brought it in to pawn, it was probably stolen or Franz had taken it in as a debt payment. Two years later when he left Mars Hill for good, he came to live with Otto and his family. He naturally went to work for Daddy Rabbit full time. Brigitta did not know what to do with him. He came home in the mornings half drunk, sometimes bleeding from a fight. He would eat the family leftovers and leave them nothing to eat. Brigitta did not know what to do; after all, he was Otto's brother. The Depression was not getting any better. Brigitta's laundry business was slowing down, and the kids were growing more and more. They needed new clothes and they ate like locusts. With Leslie going to Norfolk Navy Yard to work, Brigitta turned his old bedroom and the guest room into a suite of two rooms, a bedroom, and a setting room. She took in a couple on hard times also. They were the Carters. Mr. Carter is a druggist and the pharmacy he had opened and ran for years closed due to his customers not being able to pay their monthly bills. (A lot of grocery stores, pharmacies, hardware stores, and feed stores gave all their customers credit; so when the Depression came, most of these small stores went out of business. Mr. Carter's was one of these.] Mrs. Carter is a licensed nurse at the Anderson Hospital in West Asheville. They were a nice quiet couple. The Charleses immediately liked them. Their room and board was two dollars a week, plus Mr. Carter took care of all the Charles family's medicines. Mrs. Carter would help with the sewing. With four boys and two girls still at home, there were always a lot of mending and sewing.

By the time Albert was a senior in high school, he moved in with his grandparents in Mars Hill. He was able to finish school early and start college early. Part of the deal was Herbert and Stella would take in Albert and be responsible for his education and finances, but Otto and Brigitta would have to take in Franz.

Otto had decided that the years the family had lived in the woods had caused Franz some brain damage. Otto knew that his baby brother had eaten bugs and worms as a child and seemed to really like them. Maybe that's what caused the brain damage. Nobody could be that worthless on purpose.

CHAPTER 5

NORFOLK NAVAL YARD

Leslie was assigned the job as a welder's helper on ship plates. He liked the job very well. He liked the men he worked with. Leslie liked Norfolk—he liked the food, the music, the big city life, and the women. Leslie also liked having money in his pocket for the first time in his life. Leslie made five dollars a week. He sent five dollars a month home to his mom, and he kept the rest. He got to live in a barracks and eat in a chow hall for navy ship builders.

At this time ships were built in Newport News, Virginia. Norfolk was where the ships were fitted and refitted.

Leslie was able to play music with a couple of big dance bands and, on occasion, with the local orchestra. He fished and swam in the ocean; he played at the beach. He would hit a club or two on some weekends and danced with many of the ladies. He got to kiss and feel up some of the women. Leslie figured he had the perfect life. Within a year, Leslie was rated a welder's apprentice, another dollar a week.

Leslie worked for a master welder who was a petty officer, third class in the navy. He had been in the navy for seventeen years. All of his time in the service was at Norfolk Naval Station. His name was Billy Smith. Billy was a good man, liked to drink and fight too much or he would have been a Chief by now. Billy took home sixty-four dollars a month after deductions and expenditures. He had free room and board. If he had stayed married he would be making a little less than double that. The chief petty officer or foreman of this section of the yard started talking to Leslie about a career in the navy.

Leslie told him, "I like my life here and now. I don't see a reason to change." The chief told him to talk to some of the old salts (old navy guys) around the yard and see what they had to say.

The chief said, "This is what I can do for you. You sign up and I'll send you to the basic station at Great Lakes Naval Station in Chicago. You'll spend about twelve to fifteen weeks there, then I'll bring you back here to this yard as a welder. You'll stay here until you retire, the same as the rest of these old sailors."

"Really. You can really do that?"

"Sure, you can count on me," said the chief. Leslie signed up, and all the guys he worked with gave him all kinds of advice. Most of them gave him advice that he knew was crazy, but Petty Officer, Third Class Billy Smith gave Leslie real ideas to follow.

1. Know the eleven general orders.
2. Know all the details pertaining rank/rate recognition.
3. Learn how to make your rack (bed) with forty-five-degree corners
4. Practice ironing military creases on a long-sleeve, button-down collared shirts.
5. Read the blue jacket's manual, and pay particular attention to damage control, seamanship, first aid, uniforms, grooming, and naval history.
6. Memorize the phonetic alphabet (a list of words used to identify letters in a message transmitted on a telephone, radio, teletype, or telegraph. These are

   A-Alpha, B-Bravo, C-Charlie, D-Delta, E-Echo, F-Foxtrot, G-Gold, H-Hotel, I-India, J-July, K-Kilo, L-Lima, M-Mile, N-November, O-Oscar, P-papa,

Q-Quebec, R-Romeo S-Sierra, T-Tango, U-Uniform,
V-Victor, W-Whiskey, X-X-ray, Y-Yankee, Z-Zulu]

7.   Attend all meetings.
8.   Get in and stay in shape
9.   Try to advance to E2 or E3 (military pay grades) out of
      basic.

Leslie was in very good shape. Leslie knew the alphabet from his
dad. He also knew most of the navy rules, having worked with and
for the navy for close to the last year. Leslie decided this was a good
move on his part, so he enlisted.

In a week he was shipped to the Great Lakes Training Station
in Chicago. The navy's only basic training center and most of its
specialty schools were there also. Most of the navy schools were
inside very large buildings. They were called ships or cargo bays.
They had complete levels of ships on dry land to train on. Leslie
stored his belongings at Norfolk. He took his violin with him to the
Great Lakes. Leslie reported on board. (Even on land, you reported
on board, just like you were on a ship in the ocean.) He met men
from all walks of life. With the Depression in full swing and
unemployment, a lot of men came in so they could get a paycheck
to feed their families. A lot of the young men were married with
children. This was the only way to take care of them and learn a job.
Some of the men were running from the law or from some young
lady's family. There were a lot like Leslie—they just need a job to
help back home. There was so much unemployment that families
were losing everything. Families were being broken up and scattered
across the land. There were a few men who were hardened criminals,
who had served hard time and some who needed to be caught. But
all in all the military was a very good option. Some of these men
and their families now had health care they did not have before.
The military offered sports to play or just watch. Leslie was in great
shape and basic was not very hard for him. Leslie had worked for
the navy long enough to see how the noncoms (noncommissioned

officers) like to treat FNGs (fucking new guys), and he had seen how to act back, so none of basic training bothered him. Leslie loved to play sports, a lot of the men did. Leslie especially liked the navy version of touch football. The way they liked to play it was if you did not draw blood, you weren't having fun. Leslie hung out with young men like himself—good men, just poor.

CHAPTER 6

I'M IN THE NAVY

After eight weeks of basic training, the men started testing to see what their aptitude was in the navy to see if there were jobs in the navy for them. There was a place for everyone; they just had to find it. The last two weeks of basic training were quite nice. The men were allowed three hours a night off duty. They went to the BX (base exchange, which was like a small general store). The men went to the arcade. It had bowling, skating, movies, pool, civilian food, and beer. But the best part was they had women to talk to and dance with. Leslie was able to talk the band leader into letting him sit in on a few songs. The ladies loved it. All the recruits had pictures made and sent home. Leslie had written his folks about his decision to join the navy. He was able to send his mother fifteen dollars his first day of basic from his savings. He sent her fifteen dollars more on his third week. And fifteen dollars in three more weeks. All this money came from his savings. His last day of basic, Leslie had the navy start sending his mom twenty-eight dollars a month. This left him fourteen dollars a month. He knew he was getting a raise at graduation from basic. He was also sure he was getting the rate of E2 after basic. After ten weeks, the men starting shipping out to their rate schools. Leslie was already a fine welder, and he was given the welding test to see where he would weld.

When orders for the schools arrived, all the guys gathered around to see who got what, who liked their job and who wanted to hang themselves. Most of the men did not know what their job would be. Everything had a code and parcel names and navy names. Yeoman was a radio, teletype, telegraph, or telephone operator. (Always a good man to know. A good friend who is a yeoman can sometimes get you a call home.) A purser is a supply clerk, again always a good friend to have. Helmsmen steer the ship. Stokers, or engineers, stokes the boilers. Everybody on a ship has his real job, or rating, and then a combat job, or rating and also an emergency rating. Seaman Charles's first rating was a welder's mate. His second or combat rate was a stretcher bearer. He practiced the job daily. His stretcher crew carried Oscar around to every hatch on the ship. (Oscar is the name of the life size and weight of a male dummy.) Leslie's emergency rating was also using welding equipment to cut lose anything that would hamper a ship in combat or an emergency—a hatch, a bulkhead, railing, stairs, or anything that slowed the ship down. As all the crews graduated and began to pack up to ship out to their new duty assignments or training schools, they would go to the new school and report on board and try to find men they already knew from basic. Most of this was done within a few blocks of the basic area. Leslie carried his stuff about four blocks. He asked to come on board and was given permission to enter the barracks, sign in, and report to the duty officer, a lieutenant junior grade, J. D. Moore. The lieutenant assigned Leslie a room. This barrack was two stories tall with twelve four-man rooms, eight two-man rooms, four single rooms, and four bathrooms or heads. These had four toilets, four sinks, and a four-head shower room. There was a dayroom on each floor. The first floor had a pool table and a Ping-Pong table, a table, and chairs. The second floor had a dayroom with card tables, chairs, a couch, and a desk. Actually not a bad place to live. The Great Lakes Training Facility was just two miles above Chicago, the nation's number two city. Leslie was assigned to the welding school, but it was determined that he was advanced for that school. He was basically assigned to the regular crew welding all over the base. In the schools, you went to school the assigned number of hours a day, and then you were off duty. You had to be sober and in the uniform of the day and ready to train.

The navy expected you to attend church on Sunday mornings for the first four weeks. A trainee could not leave the base for the first four weeks of school also. After four weeks you could attend church or not, and you could apply for a pass a go to Chicago. Buses ran every half hour.

Leslie met new friends. He became friends with another welder, Charles David, an E4 or petty officer, third class (PO3); an E4 teletype operator, George Coppersmith; and an E2 who was soon to be E3, Gay Woody, a fireman. The men became fast friends. They did everything together, and they called themselves The Back Field. The guys went to the post exchange, a big variety store with groceries, the arcade, a soda shop with a gift shop, a photographer, a clothing store, and a café. There was also a skating rink, a bowling alley, a pool hall, a dance hall, and two movie theaters. On weekends it was like being at the beach or downtown in a big American city without the Depression. The navy and marines had steady money; they were young, in good shape, and there were thousands of young ladies who wanted to have fun. The north end of Chicago wanted the business and got lots of it, but it was always cheaper on base. Lots of the men did not like Chicago or they were afraid of it. These were small-town boys.

Chicago was wide open, loud, dirty, and had too much traffic and crime. The local men and boys did not like the military, although the military pours tons of much-needed money into the city. The military guys had all the money, so they naturally had all the women. Even the colored sailors and marines (these men usually had the lowest jobs—cooks, porters, launderers, most of the day labor.] had more money than the white civilians, so there was always trouble when these men went to town. A lot of men were content to stay on base to have fun. Leslie was able to get one of the band leaders who played on base at the military clubs (there were six of them—an officers' club, an NCO club, a seamen's club, a marines' NCO club, a marines' E4 and below club, and they had dances on weekends at the skating rink) to let him sit in and play sometimes. He loved it. The ladies he met loved it. What a good life. After two weeks of welding, Leslie got orders upping his rate to E3. This would be in effect in two weeks. His pay went up an additional four dollars a month. He would send two more dollars home to his mom, taking her navy money up to thirty dollars a month. Leslie kept the two remaining dollars for himself. Leslie called home to tell his family the news. His mother answered the phone. "Hello, Mom, it's me."

Brigitta happily replied, "Hello, my son. Otto, kids, come here, it's Leslie. Now, son, where are you?"

"Mom, I'm in Chicago at the Great Lakes Training Center. It looks like I'm going to be assigned here for my navy career. I'm a welder. I weld on everything. The navy has older ships to train on, and we weld on them daily. I've moved to a new barracks or ship, as the navy calls it. It's for the station's permanent party, which I'm one. I'm permanently assigned to the Great Lakes Naval Station. You and dad need to come up here to see me. Chicago is very big and has everything you ever thought of. It's cold up here. But there's lot of places to eat and things to do. Did you know that it's so cold that we do most of our training and our work inside?"

"On the inside, son? I thought you were in the navy? On a ship?"

"Mom, we train inside because of the weather. All the training buildings look like classrooms or the inside of different ships. The hatches (doors) are the same, the walls (bulkhead) are the same, the bathrooms (head) are the same, the toilets (can) are the same. All the furniture, food—everything is the same. We forget sometimes we are on dry land. I love you, Mom. Let me talk to Dad."

"Hello, son, are they feeding you right?"

"Yes, Dad, the food is fine. It's a little plain but there is a lot of it, and different too. There is chop suey from China, refried beans and rice from Panama, spanakopita from Greece, jerked chicken from Cuba. We have pineapple, cherry, pork from Hawaii, we have clam and oyster chowders form Canada. Quite an experience."

"Do you get a chance to play any music?"

"Yes, Dad. I get to play some with a couple of the local bands that play on base. I play piano and violin sometimes at the officers' club and the seamen's club. This weekend I'm going to play at the big dance club at the arcade. I'm having a good time. I left most of my belongings in Norfolk. My friend there, Billy Smith, is shipping it to me over land on a train."

"Son, do you need me to send you anything?" asked his dad. "Money or anything?"

"No, Dad, I'm fine. No, maybe tell Mom to send me some pictures of all of you. By the way, how's the kids doing? (The kids were Albert, seventeen; John Henry, fifteen; Frank, thirteen; Ava, eleven; Sonja, ten; and Little Herbert, seven.)"

"The kids are doing fine. Albert is going to College at Mars Hill and lives with your grandfather. He and your grandfather play music all day long. He loves having him with them."

"Mom said he was just so glad to get rid of Franz. How's that going?"

"Oh, it's going as good as could be expected. It's going to take time for him to adjust to living with a family again. You know he's a lot smarter than people think. Franz likes to drink, gamble, fight, has a new girl every week. He's now working full time for a Mr. Daddy Rabbit. Daddy runs an illegal bar, night club, and a bordello. Daddy also owns some buildings on Eagle Street. The colored section of town, colored-owned businesses, boarding houses, music clubs, bars, gambling. Daddy Rabbit had his finger in all these businesses, legal or not. White people do not go to Eagle Street or at least the decent white people. Franz hangs out there looking after Daddy Rabbit's interest. Franz was a collector for Daddy Rabbit. He is the collector who could go in to the white section of Asheville and collect gambling debts that a colored man could not. You do not want to see Franz at your door. It is never nice to see him. Son, you know that Franz is one of the best chefs in town. He can cook anything and make it good, especially German food. I asked him why he will not open a German restaurant. He said it would be boring and he did not think he could work any kind of regular hours. He does not want to get his clothes dirty, you know, he dresses like a dandy (a womanizer, gambler, kept man). You know that Franz sews and alters his clothes so that they fit like they were tailored for him. He always looks good, you know, son. You look just like him, but please don't act like him. Your granddad thinks Franz inherited his worthlessness from a relative in Switzerland. They say he was a count and was quite mad. Now John Henry and Frank play football at school and are quite popular with the other kids. They are both on the honor roll. The girls are both doing well in school. Unfortunately Eva is beginning to look at boys, God help us. Little Herbert is not good at school, but he seems to have the same ear for music and language as your grandfather. That boy is smart but lazy. Here's your mother again."

"Hey, Mom."

"Hey, son, son send me your address so the kids can write. Son, send us some pictures also. Have you met any nice girls? Did you meet them in church? Son, are you getting enough to eat?"

"Mom, I get all the food I can eat, and some of it is really good. Yes, Mom, I've met a couple of nice ladies in church." Leslie had only been to church the four required times and did not expect to ever go again.

Leslie's first and only year of college, he had to take Bible. The school being a church college, you had to take Bible class the first semester. He walked by the statues and paintings of Jesus every day going from Bible to the Origins of Man classes. The pictures showed a light-skinned man with long straight light-brown hair and blue eyes. The Origins of Man classes taught that you were a product of where you lived. People in the desert were dark skinned and had dark hair and eyes. The picture of Jesus was of a European. The people in the desert were Jews and Arabs. Jesus was a Jew. Leslie knew that a European born in the desert would have cooked and looked like a raisin. Leslie was also not afraid of ghosts, holy or any other kind.

He grew up playing in the Riverside Cemetery. On the hot summer nights, he and his friends would lay on the large markers naked to keep cool. Other times they would take girls to the cemetery and tell ghost stories, stories of the undead, and stories of wolflike people who looked like wolves at night but regular people in the daylight. They would snuggle with the girls, kiss them, squeeze them, touch them, but no sex. Good girls would not allow sex. They would let the boys fondle them a lot, but no sex. So needless to say, Leslie did not meet any women in church. He met them at the arcade or skating rink. Leslie met a lot of nurses at the officers' club when he played in the band but could not date them. Officers could not and would not date enlisted men.

"Son, your dad wants to say good-bye. Now you take care of yourself."

"Okay, bye, Mom."

"Son, do you get to play the piano much for the navy? Do they have pianos on ships?"

"Dad, I've never heard of a piano on a ship, especially a war ship. I don't play the piano much. I don't have one near to practice on."

"Well, son, that's a shame. Now when you're in those clubs, you're not drinking or gambling, are you?"

"No, Dad, just a beer or two for me, and I don't gamble (and he was telling the truth)."

"Leslie, I'm telling you, your uncle Franz is killing us with his antics."

"Dad, kick him out."

"Son, I can't. He's my brother, and I'm trying to help your grandfather with him. Did you know that before he came to live with us that he tried to reenlist in the army? The military would not let him back in. He must have done something awful bad not to get back into the army. He tried the President's Job Corps, but they also did not want him. So now he works for that colored gangster Mr. Daddy Rabbit. He sleeps all day, goes to work all duded up at 7:00 p.m., and gets home about 7:00 a.m. Your mother makes him pay two dollars a week for his room, and that's not enough. Everybody thinks that he got shell-shocked in the war. Nobody knows that he did not go over to the war, that he was that crazy before the war. Son, I don't think the army made him that way. He was getting into trouble his whole life, but I think the army helped it along. Son, don't let the navy do that to you. Son, when can you come home?"

"Dad, I'll come in a couple of months." Otto told his son he could ride the train from Chicago to Washington, DC, and then a train to Salisbury, North Carolina, and then to Asheville, that he would arrange it all for free. "In less than two days, you're home. You'll have to pay for your eats, so make sure you bring some bread and cheese with you. Son, do you have a teletype or telegraph on base?"

"Sure, Dad. One of my new best friends is in communications. He's a teletype operator. He plays some music also."

"Son, you can teletype me anytime I'm at lunch at work. The railroad will not care. I'll print your messages and take them home for the kids and your mom to read. We'll save a couple of bucks that way."

"Sounds good, Dad."

Otto said, "Okay, kids come and say good-bye to your brother."

Leslie could hear all the kids shouting good-bye in all kinds of different ways. He was real sure the one barking was Little Herbert. Leslie felt good and misty-eyed. His folks had good jobs, good friends, and a good place to live and bring up a family. There were rumors of war in Europe, but the navy told them it had nothing to do with them and not to worry.

Leslie went to the base's skating rink to hook up with the rest of his friends. They went into the café part of the building and ordered the same meal they always ordered—hamburger with mayonnaise, onions, catsup, and french fries all on a toasted bun, an order of onion rings, and a large beer. The entire meal cost twenty-five cents. Skate rental ran five cents. The boys all wanted to rent the skates called Chicago's. They could eat, drink, skate, and meet girls for about fifty cents a night. On this night, Leslie had on his black trousers, white starched shirt, a red bow tie, and his new black-and-gray sport coat. Man, did he look good. The other guys looked and dressed similar. Charles David had on a black shirt and a hula tie. The boys were doing well and having fun. Four women came over to the boys' booth and asked to sit with them. Yes was the answer. One of the ladies passed out some cigarettes, but the guys turned them down; none of the four smoked. The ladies all lit up and sat down.

Leslie said, "Guys, I'm going to hit the head. Does anyone need to go?" All got up to go and Coppersmith said, "Ladies, watch our seats. We'll be right back." In the head, E4 Coppersmith said, "December 2, thirty-six." E4 David said, "March 15, thirty-seven." Leslie asked what they were talking about. E3 Gay Woody said, "RHIP (rank has it's privilege)." "What does that mean?" said Leslie. Woody said, "It means that Coppersmith gets first choice of the women, and then David gets to choose, then me, and you get what's left over. That was the way it was, RHIP." Coppersmith took the one with a large gap in her front teeth and large breasts. David chose the short brunette with long curly hair and a nice body. Woody took the beautiful blonde but kind of chunky woman.

Leslie said, "NO, I don't want mine."

David asked, "Why?"

Leslie said, "She has no tits." They all laughed and went back to their table and found that their beers were drained. A waiter came to the table with a navy fireman's bucket with eight beers in it. One of the girls said, "It's the special tonight, thirty cents a bucket, and give the waiter a nickel tip." That's less than a nickel a beer with tip, not bad. And the beer was good and cold. The group drank, skated, talked, and danced in their skates. It was getting late, and the boys were on their way to getting drunk, and the women were already there. The eight of them went out for some air. It was just a little chilly. They walked over to the buses. This was a big bus stop, four or five buses at a time. The buses ran ever half hour all over Chicago. A bus came in and parked and unloaded. The bus would be in this spot for about forty-five minutes. It's the same bus the ladies could take back to Chicago. Coppersmith ran up to the bus driver and asked where he was going. "To the head, and then to get some pie and coffee."

Coppersmith asked, "If I buy you that coffee and pie, could I rent that bus for forty-five minutes?"

"*Hell no*, nobody is allowed to drive my bus. They would fire me, and I need my job, so hell no."

Coppersmith said, "No no, I don't want to drive the bus. We just want to sit in it, undisturbed for a while. You could say we just wanted to board early. I can give you four bits."

The driver finally said, "What the hell," and tossed them the keys. They boarded; the bus was still warm and dark.

CHAPTER 7

MAUDE

L eslie and his new lady, Maude (Maude did not have a job), took the back, Dave and Sissy next (Sissy worked part-time at the telephone company), and then Gay and Helen next (Helen also did not work). Coppersmith and Claude stayed in the front (Claude was a clerk at the shoe department at Sears). All the couples settled in for their desserts.

Leslie and Maude started kissing. Leslie always liked this part of a date. It made him feel manly, and he knew that someday with someone he loved he would have real sex. They kissed and kissed and fondled and touched. Maude whispered to Leslie, "Go ahead."

Leslie asked, "What?"

Maude said again, "Do it."

It was Leslie's very first time and he was so excited. When he got his thing out, it touched her and went off. He was finished and never got started. He gasped, "No, oh no." He was so humiliated he hid his face. The other guys had had women before and were having no trouble. This was his first time.

She laughed and immediately knew that it was not the right thing to do. She started cleaning both of them up. She softly told him that she knew the first time was always like this. "Please don't worry about it. Don't worry about it. I'm not going to tell anyone. It's our business only. Please don't think about it."

"You hate me, don't you?"

Maude said, "No no," and kept kissing him. "We'll get it better next time. I'll be here with my girlfriends next Friday night again. We'll meet at the same place and have a great time, believe me, I know we will." The bus driver and a bunch of passengers started lining up at the bus's door.

The four couples got off the bus and the new passengers boarded. The girls said good-bye to the boys and got back on the bus. As the bus left, the couples called back to each other good byes and I see you next week. Heading back to the barracks, three of the guys were whooping and hollering, beating their chests and sticking their middle fingers under each other's noses, saying to each other, "I'm a stud" or "You're a stud."

Leslie was miserable. He took off and said, "I'm going to the arcade for a lemonade." And he was gone. He said over his shoulder, "I'll catch up with you guys later."

"Hurry up!" shouted David.

The whole next week, Leslie tried to avoid his friends. He changed his everyday habits. He walked alone a lot, thinking of how miserable and depressed he was. How could his life have gotten so bad? Will he ever get married? Will he ever have sex? Will he ever have children? What the hell happened to him? All of a sudden it was Friday night. He stayed at work. His friends found him working. He told them he was so far behind that he shouldn't take off work.

He said, "You know, I think I'm coming down with a cold. I should go to the infirmary."

Coppersmith said, "If we have to, we're going to carry you to the arcade."

Leslie said, "Okay, let me get dressed and I'll meet you in an hour, but I don't know how long I can stay."

David said, "If you're not there in an hour, we're coming to get you."

"Okay, okay, I'll be there." Leslie got back to his room and tried to think of any way possible to avoid the evening. He knew he would have to tell the guys something they would believe. He tried to heave up his lunch, but no, it was too late for that. He stared at the phone, willing it to ring for him to go back to work. It didn't. He hoped he had gained weight and could not fit into his clothes. They fit fine. He better look if his clothes were dirty he could not wear them. They were cleaned and pressed. He was surprised how good he looked. He walked to the arcade, hoping a car would sideswipe him. No traffic tonight. "You know, I'll bet that girl does not even show up. I wouldn't if I were her, knowing I'm a eunuch." Why would she want him? He could not do what she wanted. This actually made him feel a little better. He got to the arcade, and there were his friends, and they saw him. Great. Hey, he did not see Maude. Boy, did he feel relieved. He skipped to the table, smiling, and waved to everyone. Maude's head popped up. She had picked up her cigarette from the floor. "HELL FIRE" too late, he could not run, but boy he wanted to. He hoped lightning would strike him. No such luck. You know he could have a heart attack, or maybe he could fake one. What does it look like to have a heart attack. He had never seen one, so he could not try that. Everybody at the table shifted over and he sat down by Maude. She smiled and kissed him on the cheek. As she did this, she grabbed his thing under the table. He thought he was going to faint. As he was turning bright red, he hollered, "Get me a beer. It's hot as hell in here." Maude gave him hers and laughed. A waiter came over for their orders. The girls ordered first—hot dogs, BLTs, ham salad. The guys ordered their usual. When the food came, the guys took the tops off their burgers and put on the fries and then the tops and started to eat.

Sissy, David's girl, asked, "Why do you guys put your fried potatoes in your hamburgers?"

George Coppersmith said that they had learned this from an old China sailor.

Maude asked, "What is a China sailor?"

"Sailors and marines that are stationed in China, patrolling the Yangtze River," replied Coppersmith.

"Why?" asked Maude again. Coppersmith said, "We are there to protect the Standard Oil Company and their oil."

About that time Maude gave Leslie another squeeze that made him choke on his onion ring. The group danced, drank, talked, and sang.

Gay Woody said, "It's time to go to the bus so these ladies can go home." By the time they left the arcade, Maude had squeezed Leslie about a dozen more times. His group went out and found there favorite bus driver. He said he was hungry, threw them the keys, and told them not to mess up his bus. Leslie was nervous but had a few beers in him and was very calm. The group split up as usual.

During all the kissing and fondling, Maude asked Leslie if he had ever worn a rubber. "No, I've never even seen one. Do they work?" asked Leslie.

"We're going to find out now, aren't we?" Maude told him how well he had done and how proud of him she was. This made Leslie's chest and head swell. He ran up and down the aisle, pounding his chest naked as a newborn. The group laughed and laughed. All in Leslie's life was good.

Leslie practiced his welding daily; when he wasn't practicing, he was welding. He welded on ships and on land and on trucks—big machines. He got to weld on about everything. The guys went out every Friday night. Some of the ladies changed but Leslie always had Maude. Leslie had band about every Saturday night, and the boys played sports on Sundays. Leslie and Charles David, the other welder, made all kinds of different things in the welding shop. They made hanging chimes from hanging steel pipes. Leslie had the ear for music, so he worked on each pipe until it rang in tune with the other pipes. David was better at making small picture frames. They made cupholders and plate holders. They mailed some of these home; they gave some to their girls, some to their favorite bus drivers, and some to different people on the base—band leaders and such. Boy, was life good.

Six months out of basic training, Leslie and his pal Gay Woody received orders to ship out. They were to meet an escort destroyer at the New York Navel Yard and ship to San Diego.

Leslie could not wait to tell his folks and the love of his life, Maude. "Mom, I'm going on a cruise."

"Where, son?"

"Mom, I'm going to San Diego."

"How long, son, will you be gone?"

"The cruises are usually about six months long, then back to Great Lakes or Norfolk, I don't care which. I'm going to get sea duty pay that I can save. Mom, how's everything and body at home?"

"Well, son, you know I combined Albert's room and your room and made a two-room apartment. I found some renters, the Carters. It has worked out quite well. That was such a good idea that I took the other spare bedroom and I rent it to a schoolteacher. Out of that money I was able to buy another electric washing machine. I'm doing all the laundry for the Anderson Hospital in West Asheville. The colored ladies do it. All I have to do is pick up and deliver. Your dad now has the money to get his car back on the road so he won't have to keep riding the electric trolley to work. The kids are still doing great at school. Son, we can't wait to see you."

"Mom, is Uncle Franz still with you all?"

"Oh yes, he's still here. He's here now. He's asleep. He sleeps all day and is out all night. I'm only getting two dollars a week for his room and laundry. He does his own ironing. He eats very little here. Anymore. Your dad is very concerned. Now, son, you sound so happy."

"I am, Mom, I am."

"Tell your mom all about it."

"Well, I love my life, I love my job, and I love a lady. I intend on marrying her when I'm back from the cruise."

His mom said, "Good for you, son. Tell me all about her and how you two met."

"Well, Mom, she's pretty, she's tall, and slender with long brown hair. She likes to dance, and she makes me feel like a man."

"Well, my son, how old is she?"

"Uh, I don't know. My age, I'm sure."

"And what does she do?"

"Mom, I'm sure she works somewhere in Chicago."

"Son, what is her name?"

"Maude Kennedy." Finally she had asked a question he knew. But he thought to himself, *I probably need to know some of this stuff my mother asked me.*

"Did you meet her in church?"

"Uh, well, not exactly. I met her, uh, uh, let's see. I met her on the bus to church (well, that was kind of close). We do seem to spend a lot of time on the bus."

"Well, son, we need to meet her soon."

"Mom, I'll arrange it when I get back from my cruise. I'll bring her down to meet everyone. You'll just love her."

Leslie was shipping out Monday morning (on a bus to New York and then a ship to Norfolk and then an escort destroyer to San Diego).

Tomorrow is Friday night, and I get to see my girl, he thought.

Friday, at noon, he signed off the duty station at the Great Lakes Naval Center. David also had the same orders to leave Great Lakes. They told Coppersmith and Woody that tonight was on them. They would buy the chow and the beers. They all agreed. They ate and drank and danced the night away. That night on the bus, Leslie told Maude that he had orders to ship out Monday morning and that he would be gone about five to six months. He told Maude, "I told my mom all about you."

Maude exclaimed, "What did you tell her about me? You don't know anything about me."

"I told her we were going out and that I wanted us to be together when I get the cruise over with. We can write each other every day while I'm gone."

"*No*," she said. "No, this is just for fun, that's all! I have a family."

"What do you mean a family?" Leslie cried.

"I have two children and a husband."

"Two children and you're married?" cried Leslie.

"Yes, two children and a husband. I have a boy who's thirteen and a boy that's seven. My husband is in the merchant marines. He works on an ore ship in the Great Lakes. His ports are Minneapolis to Buffalo."

"Is he okay with you coming to the base and seeing me?" asked Leslie

"He doesn't know. He ships sixteen days and then is home six days. The Friday nights he's home, I tell him I'm going to the movies with my girlfriends."

"He doesn't know about me?"

"No. Why should he?"

"Should you tell him about us?" asked Leslie.

"'Us'? what do you mean by 'us'?"

"*Us*. How we feel about each other, our plans."

"Plans? We don't have any plans. We don't feel about each other. We see each other for laughs, that's all. Look, you're a good kid. We had fun. I'm your memory for the Great Lakes, that's all. Now do you want to do *it* for the last time or not?"

Leslie got up and rushed to the door. He was out of the bus and running. He didn't know where to. All he could say was, "Damn it, damn it, damn it to hell! I love you." He walked all night around the naval base. Leslie's heart was breaking and he felt like a fool. He had to face his friends and tell them the story. Boy, was he going to be embarrassed.

It's now 8:00 a.m. Leslie and his friends always met at 8:00 a.m. for chow call to go over the night's activities. Boy, were they going to get a good laugh. He knew he had to meet them; these were the closest friends he had ever had. He and Gay were shipping out Monday morning, and the pals will not see each other for a long time. He wanted to spend some time with them. Their plans were to eat breakfast and then go to the base exchange for personal supplies, books ("crouchnovels"), stationery, candy, and gum. Then to shoot pool at the arcade, eat corn dogs, and drink a couple of beers while there. Next the bowling alley for a couple of games and another couple of beers. Back to the barracks to clean up and then to a flick, a double feature, and then go to midnight chow at the Great Lakes chow hall. (Midnight chow is the meal served to sailors who work the night shift. It's open from 10:00 p.m. and closes at 2:00 a.m. It serves regular breakfast foods and the leftovers from the evening meals. The guys loved midnight chow.) During the day's events, Leslie had to tell the guys what happened Friday night between him and Maude. The guys laughed and then saw how bad it was affecting their friend.

Charles David sat down by Leslie, put his arm on his shoulders, and said, "Leslie, let's talk."

"About what? How stupid I am? How I don't know anything? How I'm a hick from the sticks?"

"No no, Leslie, just listen to me. These ladies that come to the military bases, to our dances, skating, bowling, eating, and all the other stuff have nothing else in their lives. Times out there in civilian life are tough. People don't have jobs or money. What jobs are out there don't pay enough to live on. Some of these ladies just want to have a little fun in their lives. The men they know are in the WPA camps or in the Job Corps or CCC camps trying to make some money to support their families. Times are tough out there. Isn't that why you enlisted? Leslie, you were very lucky you met a lady that didn't take any of your money. Yes, you bought her dinner and drinks and a few cheap gifts, but look at what you got in return—a lady that taught you all about women. She did not try to trap you into marriage. She just wanted to have some fun with a nice young man. Boy, were you lucky."

His other friends told him the same thing. Leslie stayed quiet for a while, just thinking. He finally decided that they were right. He also knew he would think about Maude the rest of his life.

It's now time to go. Midnight chow was great. Leslie had pancakes, pork chops, and SOS on the pancakes. (SOS means "shit on a shingle," which is chipped beef and gravy.)

Sunday morning, up at 8:00 a.m., no breakfast, the permanent party on the base had a white glove inspection at noon on this Sunday. White glove is when an inspector, could be an officer or a chief petty officer, puts on a white glove and runs his hand over anything in the barracks to find dust. The cleaning process for this takes about an hour. There were sixteen men in each side of the barracks and a head with four toilets, four sinks, a shower with four nozzles. The barracks (ship) also had a dayroom (a large room with a couple of couches, a couple of chairs, a bookcase, two card tables with six chairs each, and a radio). The seaman would clean the barracks (ships) and some would go to church. At noon all the seamen of the barracks would be in their dress uniform, standing by their rack (bed). The chief would walk through and stop at one or two seamen and check their area. This happened every week in all the barracks. Everybody knew about it, but still there were seamen who failed the inspection. Some had on dirty or ripped or wrinkled dress uniforms, racks made wrong, dirt under the racks, seaman unshaven. Some of these men were real screwups. The chief would go outside or to the other half of the building and give the men on the messed-up side time to fix it.

This did not happen too often. Most of the men who could not adapt to this lifestyle had to repeat basic training. These men had volunteered for the navy, and the navy spent a lot of money training them. New recruits cannot just quit because they cannot learn the navy way. The navy will keep trying to train these men and find a spot for them. Some men would be put on trash detail (a job to be preformed). Trash detail means that some men will become the trash men for the base. These men would ride around the base picking up all the trash out of the trash cans on the base grounds. They would ride around on the trash trucks or the garbage ship. (At this time all the trash from the base that was not burned would be taken far out into the Great Lakes and dumped.) The sailors who had this duty or detail seemed to like it. The sailors always said that it was the best place to fish. Inspections went well in Leslie and Gay's barracks. At ten minutes after the Sunday inspection at noon, Leslie and Gay headed for the barracks (ship) that Coopersmith lived in. Coopersmith joined them and headed out, looking for their other friend. The three of them met up with Charles David on the way to the enlisted men's club. Sundays at the club was steak, boiled potatoes and butter, a green vegetable of some kind, salad, and rolls at thirty-five cents. Water, tea, coffee, or milk was free with the special. No alcohol was served on Sunday at the enlisted men's club. Families were invited. The seamen's club was not for officers, warrant officers, or chiefs. They had their own clubs. The guys ate a great Sunday lunch, and then they went to their barracks and changed clothes and got their baseball gloves, met at the diamond, and started practicing and warming up. Other sailors joined until they had enough to play a game. The game lasted about fifteen innings, as it started getting dark. The four guys headed to the arcade for their hamburgers and french fries on top. They toasted each other and had a couple beers. The night was coming to a close, and Leslie and Gay had to head back to the barracks to pack. Saying good-bye to their friends was more difficult than Leslie thought it would be. These are the friends that he became a man with, started his adult life with. He would surely miss them and the good times.

CHAPTER 8

TRIP HOME

The boys had to be on the civilian bus by 6:00 a.m. Monday morning with all their belongings. This meant they have to be on the base bus by 5:00 a.m. with their luggage. The men made it on time. As they boarded the bus to New York, they saw a couple of hundred young men just reporting into the naval basic school. They looked very young and scared.

Gay asked, "Do you think we looked that scared when we got here?"

"Probably." The boys looked to see if they could see anyone from their hometowns. The guys made their seats on the bus as comfortable as they could. Now is the time for Leslie to start his big adventure. Boy, was he ever nervous.

They boarded a bus for New York. They had three days to get there. The bus was full of sailors, all headed to their new billets (posting, new bases). Some of the men had enough time to go home for a few days before they had to report in. Every few hours the bus would stop for gas, to let people off, pick up new sailors, let everybody freshen up, eat some food, and even call home. Leslie figured that he would call home when he got to the New York City port before he boarded the new ship. He and Gay wanted to see the Empire State Building and the Statue of Liberty. Gay was from

Morganton, North Carolina, and Leslie was from Asheville, North Carolina. Both boys were like country come to town. Neither had wanted to go off base to tour Chicago, so they decided they would not miss New York. Both men had heard of pizza but had never eaten any, and they wanted to see where Babe Ruth played. It was going to be exciting. The bus rolled into New York, and the boys got their luggage and tried to figure out how to get to the Empire State Building. The boys saw a military booth and went over to ask for directions. The marine sergeant told them to go get on the blue bus, and it would take them where they wanted to go. Gay and Leslie loaded their belongings on the bus and got ready to tour New York. They were taken to the harbor of the navy billeting station. The chief petty officer of the station told them they had about one hour to get on board; the ship was getting ready to be towed out into the river.

Gay told the chief that he had another day to report. The chief ran over to Gay and put the bill of his lid (hat or cap) right in the middle of Gay's forehead hard and said, "Get on that damn ship before I corn-hole you."

"Yes, sir," they both said. The chief walked away, and the boys just stood there for a while, not knowing what to do or say.

Another seaman came over to them and said, "Men, that's the chief of the boat (ranking NCO, noncommissioned officer of the ship, usually a senior or master chief; most of the young officers were afraid of and respected the chief of the boat). You need to do exactly what he said to do. You don't want to upset him again. He can make your life a living hell."

The men said, "Yes, sir."

They reported to the duty officer at the ship, boarded, and stored all their things. There were sailors for all over America on the ship, and they came by to introduce themselves and to look over the FNGs. This ship was going to be assigned to the Philippians. Leslie and the whole crew had to work to get this ship in shipshape condition. The ship would spend five days on sea trials sailing from New York to the Norfolk, Virginia, shipyard. She would be dry-docked for two weeks. The first full day at sea, Leslie and Gay had to tour the ship. Although this was a small ship, to these two men it was very large. It was the first and largest ship either one had been on. They had to go through four fire drills that day and an "abandon ship" exercise. On board a naval ship, you have a rate and a job, but you also have an emergency job. Leslie was a welder and stretcher carrier; Gay was a fireman and only a fireman. On a ship, fires are very deadly, so firemen only has one job.

Leslie had to practice carrying a stretcher with a man in it all around the ship to find the best way to get to sick bay. The warrant officers kept closing one passageway after the other. Stretcher barriers had to learn every inch of the ship to be effective in battle. Leslie had not welded anything so far. By the end of the first day he could barely move from exhaustion. On the second day, Leslie finally got his welding assignment. He was to weld large *O* hooks to the bulkhead to pass chains through. He had eaten breakfast and was feeling and little queasy. Leslie got to his knees to start work. He remembers falling on the deck and having to pull himself to the side of the ship so he could lose his breakfast. He also got the dry heaves, his head began to hurt, and he began to pass gas. Leslie though he had been hit or shot or a fish had bitten him or that someone had poisoned him. He tried to get up but could not. A couple of his new shipmates walked around him laughing. An officer—he thinks it's a JG (lieutenant junior grade) but could not tell—said, "Mr. Charles, get up and go below."

"I can't, sir. Someone shot me!"

"Nobody shot you."

"Sir, then I'm sure someone on this ship poisoned me."

"No, Mr. Charles, you're seasick, and if you don't get up I'm going to shoot you myself. I'm taking some reports to the XO (executive officer, second in command). When I get back you better be in sick bay." The JG was gone about thirty minutes. When he came upon Leslie again, he was not happy. He kicked Leslie in the rump and asked, "Mr. Charles, what did I tell you I was going to do to you if you were still here when I got back?"

"Shoot me, sir."

"Yes, Mr. Charles, I said I would shoot you. Now you get up and go to sick bay."

Leslie said very weakly, "Shoot me, sir. I can't take any more of this." He then passed out. Day number three, Leslie wakes up in the sick bay. He's sick again. He hops up and heads for the head. He throws up again in the head. He staggers out on deck and climbs into the antiaircraft gun and goes back to sleep.

The JG finds him again. This time he tells a couple of deck hands to throw some towels on him and keep them wet. "We don't want to cook him."

Fourth day on the Atlantic Ocean and Leslie was still sick. He ate bread and drank hot black coffee. It seemed to be about the only food he could keep down. Leslie was not the only new seaman (FNG) to be sick, but he may have been the worst.

"Land ahoy," said someone, and then the XO came over the intercom and announced, "We will be in the port at Norfolk Naval Base. Put on your class A uniforms."

After the ship moored, Leslie and Gay were given nine-day passes to go home before shipping to the West Coast, to the San Diego Naval Air Station.

Leslie called his dad and told him of the pass and asked what the fastest way home was and that Gay needed a way to Morganton, North Carolina, also. His dad said for him and Gay to go to the rail yard, find the dispatcher, and tell him who they are and to make sure they are in uniform. It took the guys two hours to pack, catch a cab, and walk to the rail yard. They found the dispatcher tower and went into the office. Leslie asked for the dispatcher.

An elderly man in coveralls and a tie waved them into his office. "How can I help you, boys? Who's the Charles's kid? So you guys want to head to western North Carolina? Any of you want a drink? Got some good bourbon. What do you guys do in the navy? Are you on a ship? Y'all have to ride in a caboose and empty timber train. Be about five of you going west. You got about ten minutes to board. Nice to meet you, guys."

He was the fastest talker either one of them has ever encountered. He never even allowed them to answer a question. They ran to the train and just made it again. Leslie could tell he had lost some weight and that he looked like hell. But he was not sick anymore and was heading home to see his family. The train pulled out and Leslie went to sleep. The first stop was Highpoint, North Carolina, for fuel. All the men on the train—three in the engine, two conductors, three railroad employees, and our two sailors—got off the train for head breaks and pie and coffee. Then back on the train and off they were again. At Winston-Salem, North Carolina, the three railroad employees got off. The rest took breaks and had some coffee again. Back on board, they continued the journey. The trip takes about twenty hours. Gay got off in Morganton, which was under two hours to Asheville. Leslie was getting excited. The train started slowing, and Leslie could tell he was in Asheville. He jumped off the caboose, and there was his dad waiting on him.

"Dad, Dad, man, I'm glad to see you! Where's Mom and the family?"

Otto said they were waiting at home for him.

Leslie said, "Well, let's go."

"Get your bags, son, and I'll get the car."

"Dad, when did you get the car back on the road?"

"Well, son, your mom and I thought you may need a car to see your friends. We have told everybody we know that you are in town for a few days. By the way, son, how long can you stay?

"Dad, I'll be here for five days then I need to be back on my ship before it sails. I'm kind of excited about the cruise. We leave Norfolk to sail around Florida and then to the Panama Canal for a day, then we'll sail through it. Dad, then I'll see the Pacific Ocean. And Mexico. Places I've only dreamed of."

"Son, are you hungry? We're having turkey and dressing and all the trimmings just like Thanksgiving. I bet you that beats the navy food you been eating, hey, son?"

"You're right, Dad, except we call it navy chow. It's good and lots of it, but it's not like home cooking. Man, I can't wait."

Leslie and his dad drove into the driveway, and the whole family was there, even some people he did not know. There was his mom, his two brothers Albert and John Henry, the girls Ava and Sonja, and now he could see Frank, and there was Little Herbert. Who are the two colored women? Oh yeah, that's Ruth and her sister, Anna Laura. There were three other adults standing there with them, an elderly lady and a middle-aged couple. Leslie hugged and kissed his family.

His mom introduced him to the elderly lady first. "Leslie, this is Mrs. Bagwell. She is a teacher at Claxton Elementary on Merrimon Avenue. Mrs. Bagwell, this is my oldest son, Leslie. Leslie, Mrs. Bagwell rents a room from us. She's become one of the family. Son, this is Mr. an Mrs. Carter. They have Albert's and your old rooms. Mr. Carter is the pharmacist at the Anderson Hospital and Mrs. Carter is a nurse there also. Mr. and Mrs. Carter, this is my son Leslie."

Leslie and Mr. Carter shook hands. Leslie said, "It's good to meet you, folks."

About this time, Little Herbert yelled, "Did you bring anything from the navy for me?"

"Yes, in my bags. Now wait until I unpack." Leslie had brought the latest comic books for the boys and movie star magazines for the girls. He had a couple of Cuban cigars for his dad and a couple of very nice handkerchiefs for his mom.

Just about the time he had given out the gifts, he heard a loud rough voice saying, "Exactly what did you bring your favorite uncle?"

Leslie looked up, and coming up the stairs from his room in the basement was his uncle Franz.

"Hey, Franz, it's good to see you."

"You too, my boy, you too." Franz had on a black suit, black shirt, and a red tie with a diamond stick pin, hair all slicked back, big diamond ring on his finger, and smiling a big beautiful smile. "Hey, Sailor, come and give you favorite uncle a big hug."

Leslie hugged Franz and said, "Hey, Uncle, good to see you. You look good. What have you been doing?"

Franz answered, "Ah just doing a bit of 'reminding.'"

"Reminding? What's that?" replied Leslie.

"Well, if there is a man in town that don't know how to gamble and sometimes forgets whom he owes money to and when and don't want to pay. My job is to remind them. The hours are good, the money is good, and there's no heavy lifting." Franz hugged Leslie and whispered into his ear, "Leslie, your parents are very, very proud of you, and so am I."

The family sat down to eat the great coming-home dinner. The food looked and smelt great. They had strawberry pie and ice cream for dessert. Leslie kept them all entertained with stories of basic training, regular duty, and all his new friends. He left out the part about Maude and about being so sick on the ship. He talked about the bus ride to New York, the rail yard at Norfolk, and the train ride to Asheville. Leslie had great stories and he knew how to tell them. The hour was getting late, and so it was time to start turning in. Brigitta Charles told Leslie and Albert to bunk with John Henry and Frank. "There is going to be pancakes and bacon for breakfast."

Franz told Leslie he would see him at breakfast and that he had to go to work.

"At 9:00 p.m. at night?" asked Leslie.

"My boy," said Franz, "that's when the good life begins." And he got into his new Ford and was gone.

Otto Charles said, "Don't listen to him, son. He's not been right since he got out of the army. The sheriff of Madison County and the chief of police in Mars Hill said they had never seen a white man as mean as Franz. They said he could never come back to their towns or he would be put on the road gangs. The chancellor at Mars Hill College will have him arrested for trespassing even if he put a foot on the campus."

"Damn, Dad, I didn't know that. What happened to him in the war? Did he get gassed or shot up real bad? How bad was his wounds?"

"Son, he did not get wounded. Son, he didn't even go over to Europe and was not in any conflict. He stayed in New Orleans his two years in the army."

"Oh, that's right. I forgot," said Leslie.

"We think he honestly pickled his brain with whiskey, gambling, bar fights, and really bad women. He acts like he comes from another country or world. Son, he's just not right. He don't care if your colored, an Indian, an Oriental, or a white man or woman. He'll fight, gamble, eat, and drink with the men and sleep with the women. He just does not care. The whole town knows it too."

Leslie asked, "Dad, what does people say about him?"

"Well, son, most of the men are afraid of him, and most of the women swoon over him. It's just disgraceful. Son, I want you to make sure that you don't come out of the navy as crazy as him."

"Yes, Dad, I give you my word." But Leslie was thinking to himself, *I'll bet he has a lot of fun. Maybe I'll be just a little like him.*

The next morning, Ruth and her sister put on a great breakfast; the table was full. Otto had gotten permission to go in at 9:00 a.m. instead of 7:00 a.m. so he could have some time with his son. The family had a great breakfast. Now it's time for work and school.

Otto gave the Carters a ride to the hospital where they worked. Mrs. Bagwell had a ride to school with another teacher in the neighborhood. Albert had to catch the bus back to Mars Hill College, and John Henry and Frank wanted Leslie to go to their high school, Lee Edwards, with them. Brigitta told him to take the boys to school in her car. Leslie and the boys parked the car in front and went into the building. Leslie went into John Henry's first class with him. He met the teacher, a Mr. Noble. Mr. Noble had been in the navy in the Great War. He and Leslie talked navy for a few minutes, and then Leslie went into Frank's class and met his teacher, Ms. Scrounce (a first-year English teacher with long strawberry-blonde hair; she smelled like gardenias).

"Nice to meet you, Ms. Scrounce. Frank has told me all about you (Frank had never mentioned her)." "Well Mr. Charles, I hope he said some nice things too." "Everything he said was very good."

47

Whoa, Leslie said to himself, *that's a nice teacher. Why didn't I have a teacher like that? That kid has all the luck. I'm going to think about her today and try to figure out a plan to meet her. She's probably not like Maude, but I'll bet she's a good kisser. I could smell her three feet away. She smelled like a forest of flowers. Whoa, what pretty hair.*

CHAPTER 9

KATIE SCROUNCE

L eslie went home to pick up his mom so they could drive around and make her laundry pickups and leave the fresh, clean laundry for her customers. Brigitta and Leslie drove around town talking and window shopping.

Brigitte told Leslie, "You're going to be the head of the family one day, and you will always be the one your brothers and sisters are going to look up to. Don't be like that worthless Franz. Nobody will ever take him seriously. He's a fool."

Leslie said he understood. He felt that his folks would be around another twenty to thirty years before they would have to worry about that. Leslie and his mom pulled over at the drugstore and soda fountain on Monford. They both had Cherry Cokes. Leslie bought a box of Cracker Jacks and a note card. He wrapped the Cracker Jacks in a brown bag, licked the tape to seal it, and also taped the card he filled out on it. He gave the bag to John Henry to give to that pretty Ms. Scrounce. The card said, "Can I meet you for an ice cream and Coke at the end of school today? I'll pick you up when I pick up my brothers after school, if that's okay. Tell John Henry if that's okay."

When Leslie got to the school that afternoon, there stood his brothers and Ms. Scrounce. Leslie made the boys sit in the backseat of the car, and Ms. Scrounce sat up front with him. He drove all of them to the drugstore/soda fountain on Monford Avenue. The boys, his brothers, read comics and sat at one table, and Leslie and his guest, Ms. Scrounce, sat at another one. Leslie told Ms. Scrounce all about basic training and how he became a welder so soon He told her about his friends and the good times at the arcade on base. He left out the parts about Maude and about him being so seasick. She told him about herself. She had gone to Appalachian State Teachers College. She had been born in Granite Falls, North Carolina. Before she graduated college, her father passed away and her mother moved the family to Asheville, where her grandparents lived. Her mother was a teacher at David Miller Junior High School in Asheville. She had two younger sisters; one was still in high school, and the other was married and worked at the telephone company. She also had a brother, who was married. About that time John Henry told Leslie they were late for supper. Leslie took the boys home and then drove across town to take Ms. Scrounce home. She lived on Hilendale in the Kenilworth area of Asheville. When Leslie got home, his mom had to hear all about Ms. Scrounce.

His mom said, "Son, I see love in your eyes." About that time, Franz came into the room, saying, "I see lust in those eyes." "He's not like you. He's a good boy," exclaimed Leslie's mother.

Franz kept walking and said to himself, "Oh, I believe I'll bet you on that. He looks like me, he talks like me, he acts like me. I'm willing to bet he's a whole lot like me." Leslie and Franz ate a late supper. At 8:00 p.m., Franz asked Leslie and his dad, Otto, if Leslie could help him with a little job.

Otto exclaimed, "No!"

Franz laughed and said, "Not that kind of help. You know I wouldn't let my favorite nephew get into any kind of trouble. I just need him to drive my car. We won't be gone but about two to three hours, nothing illegal, I promise."

Otto said he did not care but told Leslie, "Watch Franz. Hanging around Franz will get you into trouble before you know it."

Leslie assured his dad he would.

Franz told him to change clothes. "Better yet, wear some of my clothes just to see if we are the same size. I promise they're clean."

Leslie put on black wing tips, black no-cuff slacks, a black belt, a gray shirt, a black tie, a black leather jacket, and a black leather newsboy cap. Franz was dressed almost the same. He had on a gray jacket and a red shirt. These guys looked good.

Franz drove him to a neighborhood called Biltmore Forest. They drove up to a very large English Tudor home. Franz got out of the car and walked around the back of the house. Leslie heard some yelling and could hear some scuffling. He ran around back to see his uncle help a man up from the ground. Franz dusted the man off and introduced him to Leslie. "Leslie, this is Mr. Dave Morris. Dave owns a restaurant in one of the hotels in Asheville. Dave, this is my nephew Les. Les is ex-military. He's my kind of a, uh, bodyguard." Dave stuck out his hand to Leslie and they shook. Franz said, "Okay, boys, let get the beast out and let's get her ready."

Leslie had no idea what they were talking about, although he liked being called Les. He liked the clothes he had on, and he liked his whole new look. He knew his parents would not like any of this. It would remind them of everything they disliked about Franz. He thought to himself, *I better store this in my brain and I'll think about it later. I need an open and alert mind hanging around Franz.* At about that time, Dave and Franz rolled out a motorcycle from the garage.

Leslie (Les) exclaimed, "What's that?"

Franz said, "My boy, this is a 1935 Indian Chief four speed, the fastest motorcycle made." The motorcycle was a two-tone green with blond leather saddlebags and a blond leather seat.

Dave said to Franz, "Now, Franz, don't hurt her. I'll win her back soon."

Franz replied, "Oh, sure you will soon. See you at Rabbit's. Les, follow me in my car." Leslie (Les) ran to the car and started it up. Franz had put on goggles, had strapped on this cap, and came roaring, motioning for Les to follow in the car. Les pulled the car as close to Franz as he dared. They sped toward Biltmore Village down

Vanderbilt Road and turned left onto All Souls Street and followed it to McDowell Street, up over the bridge and by

Lee Edwards High School (the school Leslie's brother attends), under Victoria Bridge to a right into Daddy Rabbit's (colored bar, gambling house, colored restaurant, and bordello).

They parked the car and motorcycle, and Franz gave Les a small five-shot pistol. Leslie (Les) said, "What's this for?"

Franz said, "Put it in your pocket. You're expected to carry a gun in this place. I'll let you know if you need to pull it. By the way, you do know how to shoot, don't you?"

"Oh yeah, Granddad and Dad taught us the same as they taught you. Franz, do you think I need this?"

"No," Franz said, "but you just want to be ready just in case something happens."

"What could happen? How will I know when to pull it?"

Franz said, "Les, you'll know. Believe me, you'll know." Franz and Leslie went in.

It was loud, it was hot, they were playing blues and jazz music, colored people dancing, lots of laughing and everybody drinking. Leslie saw two colored Asheville city policemen standing by a door, and there were maybe three other white people besides him and Franz in the whole place. Franz motioned him over to the door, where the colored policemen were standing.

Franz said, "Officers, this is my nephew Les. Look out for him and get him anything he wants." They stuck out there hands to shake. Leslie had never shaken a colored man's hand before. He stuck out his hand and they shook.

Franz said, "I need to take him to meet the boss. I'll catch up with you boys later."

One of the men opened the door for them and they went in. This room was also full but had plenty of white men and women. They were shooting dice on a table, playing blackjack at a table and had a poker game going at a table, and a game of tonk (a colored version of rummy) at the last table. A very slender light-skinned man with red hair and dressed in a black tuxedo walked over to them.

"Daddy Rabbit, this is my nephew Les. He's in the navy. He's staying with me a couple of days. Les, this is my boss and my good friend, Mr. Daddy Rabbit. This whole enterprise is his. I'm in charge of all of his security."

Leslie, for the third time in his life, shook hands with a colored man. His hand was strong and large and felt like rough sandpaper. Leslie liked him immediately but could tell this man was one to fear. He could see a panther in his eyes. He could tell this man was deadly. Leslie had the weird feeling of being safe around Mr. Daddy Rabbit.

Daddy Rabbit told the boys to have a good time and that he would catch up with Franz later. Leslie had a couple of beers, danced a couple of dances, ate a "salty dog" (a red wienerlike sausage in a salt pickle brim). He had a choice of pickled chicken feet, pickled boiled eggs, pickled pig's feet, salty dogs, or grilled trotters with a vinegar pepper sauce. He chose a salty dog.

A very young and pretty colored woman asked him to dance. He look around confused. She said, "Did you hear me? Do you want to dance? *Hello,* can you hear me?"

Leslie again looked around.

She poked him in the midsection. "*Hello.*"

Leslie finally said, "Am I allowed to dance with you here? Nobody is going to get upset, are they?"

"Who would get upset?" she asked.

"All the other colored men," he whined.

She laughed and said, "Where did you hear something like that?"

"I don't know," he replied.

She said, "Let's dance. I dance with whoever I want to. You can dance, can't you?"

They danced three dances. She cried, "White man, you sure can dance!" He did not want to tell her he learned some real good steps from Maude. He began to realize he had learned a lot from Maude.

Franz came over and said, "Les, it's time for me to go to work, and it's time for you to take my car home. I'll see you in the morning."

"Yes, please, Uncle Franz. I need to talk to you as soon as we can." Leslie drove Franz's car to Otto's home.

He saw a light was on in the kitchen, so he went into the home through the back door at the kitchen. His mom was having a glass of milk with a cookie, one of her prune cookies. He grabbed a glass of milk to have with her. And, of course, a couple of her prune cookies. She asked about his night. He knew to tell all that had happened but real watered down. He told her of his eating a salty dog and having a couple of beers and dancing. He left out the part where he danced with the colored girl. He told her he had met a friend of Franz who owned a restaurant. He didn't tell her that Franz had to smack the man around a bit first. And that Franz had taken the man's motorcycle over a gambling debt.

The next morning Leslie was up early and had written another note to Ms. Scrounce, asking her if she would let him take her to dinner that evening. He would pick her up at 7:00 p.m. and have her home by 10:30 p.m., if that was okay with her mother. He told her to please let John Henry know today at school. He had breakfast with his mom and brothers and sisters. Otto had to be to work at 7:00 a.m. each morning. He told John Henry and Frank to get into the car, that it was time for school. Ava and Sonja wanted him to take them to school also. They said, "You can drive right by it on your way to take the boys." Little Herbert would be walked to school by his mom.

As Leslie headed out the door, the phone rang. Ruth picked up the phone. "Charles's residence. Mr. Leslie, this call is for you."

"Hello, this is Leslie."

"Nephew, it's Franz. I need your help."

"Sure, Franz, what can I do for you?"

"Listen and keep this quiet. I'm hurt and need you to pick up some bandages and come and get me."

"What happened?"

"I'll tell you later, come on."

"I have to take the kids to school then go to the drugstore then I'll be there."

"Just hurry."

"To Mr. Daddy Rabbit's?"

"No, come to Birdeye Plemmons Cafe on River Road. Do you know where that's at?"

"Yes, sir, I'm on the way." Leslie took his sisters to David Miller Junior High School and the boys to Lee Edwards High School. He gave John Henry the note to Ms. Scrounce. He picked up first-aid supplies at the drugstore and headed toward the river. All the boys and girls in downtown Asheville knew how to get to Birdeye place. They all got late-night hot dogs and hamburgers there and, every now and again, could talk a waitress into serving them beer.

Birdeye Plemmons controlled most of the gambling in the city of Asheville. He owned a truck-stop café on River Road.

As soon as Leslie drove up, he saw Franz, Daddy Rabbit, and a short bald round man with a cook's apron on. Franz was bleeding from the top of his head. Daddy Rabbit had bled through his nose and had blood all over himself. Birdeye stuck out his hand to Leslie and Leslie shook it. Birdeye laughed and reached this time for the bandages.

Leslie asked, "What happened?"

Birdeye answered, "They went to buy a couple of slot machines behind the Glen Rock Hotel and were jumped and robbed." Franz was drinking bourbon and by now was real mellow. Birdeye patched the men up, and Leslie loaded them into the car and headed home.

Daddy said, "Take me to the club. I live upstairs." Leslie took Daddy home. He now headed toward his folks' home.

"Franz, can we talk?"

"Sure, kid. What do you want to talk about?"

"Well, to start, I had a great time last night."

Franz said, "I knew you would, Les. You're a lot like me. We could be twins."

Leslie asked, "How did I do? What did anyone say about me?"

"Les, you did just fine."

"You know, Franz, I had never touched a colored person before."

"Well, Les, was it any different? Did any color rub off on you?"

"No, that's not what I mean. They acted a lot like us at parties, and no one seemed to care if I danced with a colored girl. Boy, was she nice to dance with."

"Les, what did you really expect?"

"I don't know. I've always been told different stories about colored people."

"Les, it's time you learned about life and people for yourself. Les, now get me home. I've got to get some sleep. By the way, nephew, what are you planning to do today?"

"I'm going to take Mom on her rounds and then pick all the kids up at school, including Little Herbert. Then I'm going to dinner with Ms. Scrounce."

"Boy, that sounds pretty good, or at least the dinner part does. How about I get a date and take both of you out, my treat. We'll go to Dave Morris's French Restaurant. The food is very good. Come on, we will have a couple of laughs."

"Okay, sounds good to me." When Leslie got Franz home, Franz had fallen asleep. Leslie woke him up, and he had to help Franz stagger quietly down to his room.

At about 6:00 p.m., Franz came into Leslie's room with some clothes for Leslie to wear—black wing tips, black slacks, black belt, white shirt, a dark-red tie, and a gray sport coat. Franz was dressed similarly. The men headed out in Franz's car. Franz told him to pick up Ms. Scrounce, and they would meet his date at the restaurant. She works there in the evenings. They parked on the street on Broadway and went in to the Langran Hotel. It was fancy and large. They walked over to the hostess's desk to be seated. A beautiful woman, about thirty, came over to greet them.

Franz said, "Les, this is Mrs. Suzie Davis, my date. Suzie, this is my nephew Les and his date, Ms. Scrounce. Ms. Scrounce is a schoolteacher."

Suzie said, "Nice to meet all of you. Follow me to your table." The three of them sat as Suzie went to get menus.

Franz said, "She's a widow. Her husband fell off of a bridge and broke his neck."

"Whoa," said Leslie, "and he broke his neck."

"Yeah," said Franz, "and I was there when it happened and so was her brother."

Les (Leslie) had a strange feeling in his stomach after hearing that.

Suzie joined them and asked, "Ms. Scrounce, what do you teach?"

"I teach English literature to the sophomores and seniors at Lee Edwards High School."

"How did you two meet?" asked Suzie.

"Leslie is the older brother of one of my students," replied Ms. Scrounce "How long have you two been dating?" asked Suzie.

"Oh, this is our first real date," said Leslie. "How about you and my uncle Franz? How long have you known each other?"

"Franz and my brother have been friends for a couple of years, I think. I met him after my husband died."

"Ms. Scrounce," asked Franz, "how do you like being a teacher?"

"I would like for all of you to call me Katie. That's my first name, and I just love teaching English lit."

"How long are you home for?" asked Suzie to Leslie.

"I have to leave on Thursday, that's two days from today."

The waiter brought them their food. They had tiny little flat pancakes folded over. It had cubes of beef and mushrooms on top with a very thick red wine sauce. They had a baked pear with nuts and cinnamon, little tiny cabbages called brussels sprout with a pepper butter sauce, something call celery root, potatoes au gratin, which was very good, and a little black roll rolled in seeds.

Leslie had never tasted anything as different or as good. Ms. Katie Scrounce said the same. The four of them laughed and talked and had the best time. A great evening to remember.

It was a few minutes after ten when Les said, "I have to take Katie home, although I wish I could keep her forever." She hugged him and kissed him on the cheek.

Suzie said, "Well, it looks like I have to go to work. It was nice to meet the both of you. Let's promise to do it again."

Franz said, "Drop me off at the club."

Leslie dropped Franz off at the club. Leslie took Katie home and got there at exactly 10:30 p.m. Katie asked Leslie if he would like to sit on the porch and have a glass of tea.

"Yes," whispered Leslie. "I would love to," he again whispered.

Katie asked, "Why are you whispering?"

"I didn't want to wake your mother."

"Leslie, my mother is sitting right there by the window," she laughed.

Leslie felt a little foolish, and he could feel his cheeks getting warm and red. He kind of laughed too. Katie got them some tea, and they set on the steps of the porch and quietly drank their tea. Leslie felt warm and nice sitting there with her. He could smell her and she smelled really nice.

The screen door of the house opened, and Katie's mom peeked out and said, "Katie, I'm going to bed. Don't you be too long. Nice to see you again, Mr. Charles."

"It's good to see you, Mrs. Scrounce," he replied.

As soon as the light in the front room went out, Leslie bent over and kissed Katie; she kissed back. They kissed and hugged each other for a few minutes. Katie was breathless and warm all over. She told Leslie that she had to go in or her mom would come and get her.

Leslie asked, "When can we go out again? I only have two days left."

"We could go to a movie, and then we could eat at the soda shop tomorrow, if would like to?"

"Yes!" he exclaimed. "Yes yes."

She kissed him again and said, "Where are you going now?"

"I have to take Franz's car to him, I think," he replied. Leslie danced to the car and headed to Daddy Rabbit's.

Les went into the club. The door man said, "How you doing, Mr. Les? Looking for your brother?"

"My brother? No no, that's my uncle. Have you seen him?"

"Yeah, he's in the private room. Come on, I'll take you in."

"Lead the way," said Leslie. Leslie saw his uncle and Daddy. Daddy had a swollen nose and swollen purple eyes. They waved him over and gave him a beer.

Daddy Rabbit said, "I heard you was trying to get some learning, is that right, boy?" He laughed the whole time, winking at Leslie.

Leslie said, "What do you mean, sir?"

Franz stepped in and said, "He knows your dating a teacher, that's all." He laughed.

About that time, Dave Morris came over to him and asked about dinner.

Leslie said, "It was the best chow I've ever eaten. I don't even know what some of that food was. Your sister was real nice too. And Katie also thought she was real nice."

"Yeah, she's a good kid, just can't pick men."

Franz came up and said, "Let's go." Leslie knew not to ask where. He and Daddy Rabbit and Franz got into Franz's car. "Les, you drive," said Franz.

"Where to?" said Leslie.

"Do you know where Creeds Bar on Haywood Road in West Asheville is?"

"Yeah."

"Then let's go there."

When they got to the front of the bar, Franz said, "I'm going into the bar. Les, you drive to the back alley. I'll meet you there. Daddy, you got your new toy?" Daddy Rabbit giggled and said he did. He pulled out a Thompson .45 caliber submachine.

Leslie asked, "Where did you get that?"

"From a cop friend of mine," replied Daddy.

Franz went into the bar and screamed, "Where's Joyner and Blalock?"

As Daddy Rabbit and Leslie pulled to the back of the building, two men ran out the back door and started getting into a car. Daddy Rabbit jumped out of Franz's car holding the Thompson straight down at his side. Leslie got out on his side of the car. At that time, the Thompson starting firing. Daddy was only holding it with one hand. It spun Daddy around and he shot Franz's car (two holes in the back passenger door). He kept turning and hit the other car that the two men were trying to get into. The bullets hit the car and the driver maybe about a dozen times. The passenger of the car jumped out and starting running down the street. At that time Franz came running out of the bar, chasing the passenger.

Leslie jumped behind Daddy Rabbit and grabbed his gun hand and held the Thompson straight up in the air until it was empty. He looked at Daddy Rabbit and then they both heard two shots.

Franz came running up to them and said, "LET'S GO!"

The men jumped into the car and sped away. Daddy said, "Damn, I grabbed hold of that damn thing and it would not let go of me. Thanks for grabbing that damn thing for me.

"Whoa," exclaimed Franz, "was that fun or what?"

Leslie asked, "Where do we go next?"

"Take us to the club and you can go home."

"How are you going to get home?" asked Leslie.

"Les, did you forget about my motorcycle? It's still here at Rabbit's."

"Les, Franz told me you play a mean violin. Is that true?"

"Yes, sir."

"When do you play and where?" asked Daddy.

"I play at the train station at lunch so my dad and I can play together. He plays much better than me."

"I'd like to hear you sometime. What kind of music do you play?"

"I play all music, but I like swing and big band music best. You know, something with a beat."

"Yeah, man, I got you," replied Daddy Rabbit.

They got to the club and Daddy Rabbit and Franz got out. Franz leaned over to Leslie and said, "Please don't tell your folks what we do when you're with me."

"No worries," said Leslie, "I'm not about to tell anyone what we did." As he was driving home, Leslie had to pull over because he was shaking so bad. He kept thinking to himself, *What the hell happened? Mr. Daddy Rabbit could've killed us with that Thompson. He didn't even know how to handle it. I don't know how to shoot a Thompson either. Those other two shots, what were they? Was Franz involved in that? What happened to the other man? Why didn't we try to help the man Daddy Rabbit accidentally shot? It was an accident, wasn't it? I don't want to think about it. I want to think about my Katie.* He began to feel warm thinking about Katie. He drove on home and turned in.

The next morning Leslie got up and took all his brothers and sisters to school. He gave John Henry another note for Katie. He thanked her for the last evening and told her he was counting the minutes until he would see her again.

Leslie's mom told him to drive to Mars Hill College and see his grandparents while he had a chance. He headed straight to the college. The drive would take him a little over an hour. When he got to the college, he drove straight to his grandparents' home, which was one block off of the campus. His grandparents both worked at the college, and both were very well respected. His grandfather, Herbert Charles, was a music teacher and the maintenance man of the musical instruments. His grandmother was the head cook at the women's dorm and cafeteria. Both were so glad to see him. Stella fed him great German food and the three of them played music. Leslie told them of Katie Scrounce and his love for her. His grandfather gave him a lap steel Hawaiian guitar. "Son, while you're on that ship, you can learn to play this Hawaiian guitar."

"Granddad, I had a friend who had one of these at the Great Lakes, and I picked at it some. They sound pretty good." His granddad pulled out the camera and they took a lot of pictures.

"Now, Grandmother, mail me some of those pictures when I'm on the ship."

Stella Charles told her grandson, "Honey, I sure will," and hugged Leslie good-bye for a while.

He left Mars Hill, heading for Asheville and his Katie. He bathed and got dressed in some more clothes that Franz wanted him to wear. Brown and white Oxford shoes, brown socks, brown pleated cuffed slacks, white shirt, a dark-chocolate cashmere armband cardigan, and a nice cream-colored fedora

As he left the house, Franz said to come by the club that night. Daddy Rabbit has a present for him. When he walked on the porch at Otto's home, all the kids started singing, "Leslie and Katie setting in a tree, k-i-s-s-i-n-g. How many kisses did he kiss her?" With every step he took, they all counted, "One, two, three, four, five, six . . ." until he got into the car and left.

He and Katie saw a singing cowboy Western; neither could tell you what it was about. After the movie, they went to a soda shop on pack square and ordered. Leslie had a hot dog and a grilled cheese sandwich with french fries and a Cherry Coke. Katie had a BLT, fries, and a Dr. Pepper. They split a banana split for dessert. They held hands, laughed, and talked. Leslie pulled out his Hawaiian guitar and played her some songs. He played and she sang. She really had a great singing voice. Boy, were they having a good night.

It was almost 10:30 p.m., and Katie said, "I have got to get home."

Leslie took her home about ten minutes late. Her mom was at the window looking out. Her mom just looked at them and turned off the main light and went further into the house.

"Wow," whispered Leslie, "is she upset?"

"She's fine, Leslie, but I'd better get in." She grabbed him and kissed him long and hard.

Leslie asked, "Will you come to my folks' home for supper tomorrow night? They're giving me a good-bye dinner, and I really want you there."

"Yes," she said, squeezing his hand and pressing her body as close to him as possible.

"I'll pick you up at six, if that's okay?"

"That's fine," she replied. They kissed again and Leslie left. He again felt warm and very good. He headed home when he remembered he had to stop at Daddy Rabbit's.

Leslie knocked on the door of the club and was ushered in by the doorman. His uncle saw him and waved him over.

"I'll let Daddy know you're here. Order us a beer and I'll be right back." The beers got to the table the same time Daddy Rabbit got there.

"Good to see you, Les," said Daddy Rabbit as he shook Leslie's hand.

"Good to see you also, sir," replied Leslie.

Daddy Rabbit laid a large box on the table and said, "To show you my appreciation for saving my life from that damn gun. I hope you like it."

Leslie opened the box. In it were two white shirts, a red and a gray tie, and a black suit with an extra pair of pants that were gray.

"They should fit fine," said Franz. "I tried them on."

"Thanks, Daddy Rabbit. You didn't have to do this."

"I know. That's why I did it," laughed Daddy Rabbit.

"My folks are giving me a going-away-for-a-while dinner at their home tomorrow night. Would you like to come?" asked Leslie.

Daddy Rabbit laughed again and said, "Son, I would love to come, but you know I can't."

"I'll explain it to you later," said Franz. "Would you mind if I brought Mrs. Suzie Davis with me? I am invited, aren't I?"

"Absolutely," replied Leslie. "You know you are, and Katie is coming also. We'll have great fun."

"Very good," said Franz. "Now get on home before the folks blame your being late on me."

Leslie drove home feeling even better than before, if that were possible. He had a good sleep, thinking about Katie the whole time.

Leslie got up early and took all the kids to school; he took his mother on her rounds. He then went to see his dad and took him his lunch. He took his new Hawaiian guitar with him, and he and his dad played some music.

His dad was very good on the guitar. They played and laughed and had a good time. Leslie picked his siblings up from the schools and headed home. He stopped by the florist on Charlotte Street and picked up some flowers. When he got home he gave his mom half the flowers and saved the rest for Katie's mom. He put on his new clothes given to him by Daddy Rabbit. Boy, did he look good. About 6:15 p.m., he headed for the Scrounce home with flowers in hand. He didn't have to knock. Katie had the door open waiting for him. "Good afternoon, Mrs. Scrounce, it's so nice to see you. What time should I have Katie home?"

"Ten thirty would be nice," she said.

"Yes, Mrs. Scrounce. We'll be here by ten thirty."

"Okay, you kids have a good time," she said. Leslie turned to leave when he realized he still had the flowers in his hand. He gave them to Katie and said, "These are for your mom." Katie laughed and took them in to Mrs. Scrounce. Leslie and Katie got to Otto's home at six forty-five. Everybody was there—his parents, his brothers and sisters, his grandparents, the three boarders, and he and Katie. He introduced Katie to the family and boarders. Everybody was standing and talking when Anna Laura came out of the kitchen and said, "Ruth said we goanna start serving in five minutes. Please come to the table."

Franz and Mrs. Suzie Davis came into the house. Everybody just looked. Franz had never brought anyone to the house. Katie went to Suzie and hugged her and said, "I'll introduce you to Leslie's family." Otto and Brigitta welcomed her to the home when they were introduced. They looked at her and then to each other. People married this long could look at each other and know what the other was thinking. She was nice—she dressed very nice, she had good teeth, very little makeup, her hair looked clean and nice, and she talked educated. Where did he find her? Does she know who and what he is?

"Let's all go to the table and sit, Ruth, whenever you're ready," said Brigitta.

The food was great. Two big chuck roasts, gravy, whole boiled potatoes, greasy cut short beans, stewed pearl onions, sliced cucumbers and sliced Tommy Toe tomatoes in cider vinegar, stacks of fried corn bread the size of pancakes, maybe thinner, with butter on them, and lots of unsweetened tea. For dessert, they had apple cake and coffee. Everyone ate and talked.

When Ruth came out to start clearing the table, Brigitta said, "Let's go to the music room for more coffee." Otto picked up a guitar, Herbert sat at the piano, Leslie pulled out his Hawaiian guitar, and John Henry, the violin. They all played and sang. Little Herbert had a small drum he beat and stayed in time with the rest. Brigitta kind of cornered Suzie Davis and pumped her for information, like what she did for a living. She worked for her brother at the restaurant since her husband passed away. "Oh, I'm so sorry. What happened?" "He fell one evening hunting with my brother, Dave Morris, and Franz and a man named Buddy Bryant. He stumbled and fell from the Beaumont Street Bridge." Otto had told Brigitta that a friend of his at the rail station said Franz had thrown a man off a bridge over gambling debts a few years ago. She really did not believe it, until now. Brigitta said to herself, *Suzie, you poor child, run. If you know what's good for you, RUN.*

Brigitta asked, "Suzie, what do you do at the restaurant?"

"Oh, I keep the books and I'm the hostess at night. You need to come and eat with us. Our food is not as good as what we just had, but it's close."

Brigitta said, "Thank you, we just may do that." Brigitta liked her immediately. But she still could not see why she was with Franz.

65

At a quarter before ten, Leslie said, "It's getting late and I have to take Katie home."

As they left, the kids started sing again. "Leslie and Katie sitting in a tree, k-i-s-s-i-n-g . . ."

Leslie hurried her into the car and left. She started laughing. She asked him to pull over on Kenilworth before he turned on Hilendale.

She slid over to him and said, "How many kisses did he give her?" and kissed him. He slid to her also. As they kissed, she turned and faced him. She scissored her legs between his and started kind of humping his leg like he had seen dogs do.

He was hard and hot.

She whispered to him, "I love you."

And he said, "I love you." They kept kissing and humping. He slid his hands under her and up her dress.

She stopped and could barely catch her breath and said, "We can't, not here, not like this. I'm a good girl. I want this to be story-book great. Not in a car. I love you."

"I love you too. We can wait until I get back," Leslie said.

"Will we get married then?" she whispered.

"If that's your wish."

She said yes, and they kissed long and hard. And he got her home by 10:30 p.m. As he drove into his mom's driveway, there stood Suzie and Franz talking to the Carters, the boarders. Leslie went over and joined them. The Carters told him how much they enjoyed meeting Katie. Otto and Brigitta came out of the house to join them.

Franz and Leslie walked into the shadows. They talked about why Daddy Rabbit could not come to the dinner. Franz explained, "Daddy is my best friend as well as he's my boss, but he and I both know we cannot hang out together in this town or any small Southern town. Colored and white people don't mix, not allowed to mix. Maybe someday, not in our lifetime, but someday."

Suzie called over, "Franz, I need to get home."

"Okay, dear," he replied. And they left.

Brigitta asked Leslie, "How serious are they?"

"Don't know, Mom. This is only the second time I've seen her," Leslie answered.

"You know, he may be human after all," she said.

Otto said, "I've got to leave at six forty-five in the morning. I've got to go to bed. Leslie, get packed up so we can leave on time. Your train pulls out at 7:20 a.m. You're going to haul lumber to Highpoint. You'll change trains in Highpoint, North Carolina, and get onto the passenger train from Florida to Norfolk. Your friend Seaman Woody is on the same train."

"That's good, Dad, thanks."

CHAPTER 10

///

CHINA SAILORS

There are four main groups in China, and they are starting to clash daily somewhere in the country. The Japanese are fighting the Communists, who are fighting the nationalist army. The warlords alienated themselves with Chiang Kai-shek's nationalist armies. The Europeans are clashing with the nationalists and the Communists, while the Americans are trying to stay neutral but are threatening sanctions. The Second Sino-Japanese War has started. The Japanese have occupied Korea since the First Sino-Japanese War. The United States has now put gunboats in the Yangtze River for the protection of American interest, American life, and American property and to further American goodwill in China and the Yangtze River and its tributaries. The Americans did not, at this time, care who won the wars as long as they stayed friends with the winner.

The crews of the gunboats were called China sailors or "the pirate-fighting river rats." These were very tough men and crews. They were allowed to grow beards and carry weapons. All sides in this conflict were trying to control the river and its lands. There were so many pirates and warlords you could not readily tell whose side they were on. Most of the time they were only on their own side.

The American-owned Standard Oil Company was screaming to Congress to protect them better. They were tired of paying every river pirate a toll and losing crew members at every port. They wanted Congress to send porters or coolies (cheap labor, laborers who could be worked half to death—no one cared if they complained—laborers who could be kept segregated from the Chinese). They wanted American colored men or Filipino men. Congress could not figure out how to do that legally. The best they could do was add a couple more gunboats to the river command.

Standard Oil and the America West China Company were complaining daily to Congress that other countries had increased their presence in the area, why not the United States? They wanted the United States to send troops and lots of them.

At this time in history, the United States and Japan had a good relationship. The Russians were supplying the Communists. Japan was trading with the United States. China was not a friend of the Americans. Our government figured that Chiang Kai-shek's nationalist army could not win, and we did not want to back the loser. We were in China only to protect our own interest. We increased our presence in the East China Sea with newer escort destroyers, Mahan-class, 1,500 tons, carrying 205 men and 35 officers and about 20 Filipino porters. And the United States added two gunboats last year. They were the USS *Luzon* and the USS *Oahu*. Two older gunboats six months ago, they are the USS *Panay* and the USS *Mindanao*. Last month the United States Navy added two more gunboats, the USS *Guam* and the USS *Tutuila*. These boats looked like Mississippi riverboats. They were flat bottomed and well armed. Each boat had a crew of sixty-five to eighty men and ten officers. They also carried about twenty coolies or porters. These were Chinese men whose jobs were to do all the laundry, cooking, cleaning, polishing. They do all the loading and unloading of cargo and supplies.

The American sailors on these ships had the best duty in the navy. They sunbathed, gambled, read, and generally had an easy life. Most of them had Chinese wives and families in two or three different ports on the Yangtze River that they patrolled. They also patrolled the Kiagsu and the Chekiang rivers. The Yangtze was a little over 1,300 miles long. Sometimes these sailors were out of their port for weeks. They had plenty of money. It was so cheap to live in China, and they lived like kings. To keep a wife and home in a little port up the river was about three dollars of month. It was cheap enough to have more than one wife. The escort destroyer sailors were not so lucky. They were based out of Shanghai, which at that time was one of the world's most cosmopolitan cities. Shanghai had a population of three million Chinese, making it the world's fifth largest cities. It had a foreign population of about three hundred thousand. Although not expensive, it still costs almost double the rest of China to live there. Shanghai was famous for its shopping, trading, and opium.

On December 12, 1937, the Japanese attacked two cargo ships and the USS *Panay* and Nanjing on the Yangtze. The Japanese sank three of the boats. There were two news reporters on the ships and they filmed the incident. The Japanese government swore it was an accident done by one lone plane and the pilot did not see an American flag. The film told a different story. It showed four planes, and it showed the flag very prominently waving. The Japanese government gave the United States $2.2 million and apologized—this only after the United States started sanctions against Japan. The United States felt this was an imperialistic act of aggression and starting arming at the nationalist army.

Leslie and Gay Woody arrived at Norfolk on a beautiful Saturday morning in September. They reported to their ship. The ship looked ready to go to sea and she did on Sunday morning. Leslie dreaded it. He was told the sickness would come back as soon as they lost sight of the coast. He began to feel the queasiness coming on. He got a cup of water and put a powder in it and drank. Mr. Carter, the druggist, had made him seven powders, one for each day he felt sick. He said it was for women who had morning sickness. It must have worked because he began to feel okay. All of his shipmates had a pool as to when he would throw up. Sea duty was now okay. He could eat as long as it was not greasy. He ate lots of vegetables, bread, cereal, no sugar, and black coffee or unsweetened tea. He was able to eat a little more as each day passed. His work was fine. He spot welded things all over the ship. He learned to play tonk, rummy, and dollar checkers. Leslie had always played chess with his father, granddad, his mother (who was the best player in the family), brothers, sisters, and uncle Franz. Franz taught him to cheat in all games. He didn't do it but knew how, and he knew how to catch others. He wrote a continuing letter to his mom and to Katie daily, a page a day, and mailed it weekly.

The ship went down the East Coast and made its first stop in Cuba to resupply. The men were going to be allowed the four days they were in port to sightsee. They were in Cuba only two days. The ship then cruised to the Panama Canal. The ship had to wait twenty-four hours before it was allowed to go through the locks. The crew mostly stayed out on deck and watched their passage through each lock. Leslie played his guitar and violin about every day. There were plenty of sailors with instruments on board. The guys liked to play and sing. Gay Woody took guitar lessons every day from one of the other firemen on board. He wasn't that good but he tried. They sailed into the Pacific Ocean and turned north for San Diego, one of the largest naval ports on the West Coast. Leslie and Gay had planned to room together while in port. They planned on taking in all the sights in California and Mexico. The boys planned to save up leave time and hop a freight home again. With fifteen days they could travel five days and be home for ten days. They planned on doing that in three months. Leslie wrote Katie and told her his plan. On the second trip to Asheville he and Gay would make, about six months from now, he and Katie could get married. They could stay at his folks' home on their honeymoon, and she could move back in and stay at her mother's the rest of the time he was in the navy. He could save twenty dollars a month, and she could save ten dollars a month. With extra monies he could make playing music, they would have a nice nest egg to start their lives with. He would go to work at the roundhouse at the rail yard in Asheville as a welder, and she could teach. They would have the best life. Her return mail affirmed her love for him and she loved his plans.

Her new best friend, Suzie Davis, was going to help plan the wedding and make the dresses. She also knew they would have the best life together. Leslie was sending her money and she also saved.

The ship docked and the men left the ship. Gay and Leslie went to the enlisted men's barracks to get a room. They were told to report to the transient barracks. The transient barracks was open bay, twenty-two men and no dividing walls. Each man had a clothes locker and a foot locker, a floor lamp, and a single cot. They had the same posted rules as they had at Great Lakes—once-a-week inspections, no drinking, no gambling, no women, no fighting. They had the same chow except they had more juice, more fruit, more fish—all in all, a pretty good place. The first morning at Santa Diego Naval Station, the new men reported to the base welcoming center. They each signed in at personnel, at the chapel, at payroll, at the hospital, at the Red Cross, and finally at their new duty stations. Leslie was told to report the next morning at 0600 hours (6:00 a.m.). He was given a welding test to see what he knew and how well he could do it. He passed his proficiency test with flying colors. Leslie and a chief were given the task of welding a steel barrier around a machine-gun emplacement on an escort destroyer. The destroyer had nine machine guns, and they all needed the barriers welded in. Leslie and the chief had to add two new gun emplacements with steel barriers. Leslie was informed that he would have thirty days to get this task done. This included sanding and painting. Leslie was given orders the next day promoting him to E4. This gave him a raise of eight dollars a month. *Boy* Leslie thought to himself, *things are looking up for me*. The next morning when he got to work, he was given new order to board the escort destroyer he was working on as part of its full crew. The ship was going to the East China Sea the next day at 0600 hours. Leslie saw his friend Gay and told him of his good and bad luck. Gay had not got promoted, and he was going to stay in San Diego. Leslie knew he had to rush to get signed off the base and go to payroll to have thirty dollars monthly sent to Katie Scrounce for their savings account. He called his folks and Katie and told them the news. He was told the ship would be back to San Diego in four months, and he told them this also. He also told them he would be on leave at that time and could come home for a couple of weeks. Leslie boarded his new ship, and it pulled out of port in a real bad storm. The bad weather lasted three days. Leslie could not work during that time. He played cards with the other sailors and drank a home brew on the ship called raisin jack. (Raisin jack was made from fermented raisins mixed with sugar and water.) It would sit you on your ass if you drank too much. Leslie drank it to keep from getting seasick. He was sick anyway, but it was from the raisin jack. This was the first time Leslie had been drunk and then sick and then hung over. The rest of the cruise, Leslie welded and played his guitar. He made some new friends on the ship. The chief he worked for was a longtime sailor who had been around the world many times. He had been in most navy ports and was a good man. His name was Joe McGhee. He told Leslie that the ship was built in the Great War. These ships were called tin cans. They traveled in packs, usually three to five ships in a group. Their job was to hunt down U-boats and to be the first in on a fight. They had .38-caliber and .50-caliber machine guns, torpedo tubes, depth charges, and five three-inch guns. They were expendable. They were to protect the larger ships. The cruse was a pretty easy cruise. Leslie knew his job and he did it well. The ship had four new movies and four older movies on it, two new Charlie Chans, two new Westerns, two mysteries, and two comedies. The captain showed two movies a night. All the men could act out all the movies by heart by the time the cruise was over. Thirty days into the cruise, they saw the coast of China. Before they could dock, another storm rolled in. The ship sailed up the china coast and back for five days until the storm had blown itself out.

In port, the crew finished off loading the ship, and so the crew got to take a little holiday. The crew got twelve hours on duty and twelve hours off. The chief took Leslie on a tour of Shanghai. Sights, sounds, smells, people—all new and exciting. He heard all kinds of languages, and on occasions he even heard German.

The captain let the men work for four hours and then eat and sleep for eight hours. And then they could leave the ship to tour the city for twelve hours. They had to follow a few simple rules: (1) they cannot come on the ship drunk, (2) they cannot bring anyone on the ship, (3) they cannot bring animals on the ship, (4) each sailor had to be at work on time and sober and in uniform, and (5) the ship had to have two officers and forty enlisted men on duty at all times.

Shanghai was a very large modern cosmopolitan city. As the Sino-Japanese War continued, Shanghai kept getting larger. The war was not affecting Shanghai except for the refugees. Shanghai was a wide open city—drugs, women, money, slavery, warlords, and every crime you could think of. You could buy anything—clothes, china, cars, jewelry, cameras, radios, people, exotic animals. If you could think of it, you could buy it in Shanghai. Leslie bought four yards of white silk and four yards of pink silk. He mailed the white to Katie and the pink to his mom. He mailed six silk ties to his dad and his brothers and his uncle Franz. He mailed his sisters silk scarves. Leslie decided since he was in China he might as well try to mail it home. He told the chief of the French food he had eaten in Asheville, so they decided to find a French restaurant and try the food. Shanghai, being an international city, had restaurants with cuisines from every country and city in the world. The first French restaurant they found would not let them in. They had a dress code—coat and tie and no uniforms. They also could not read the menus. They were in French. When they found another French eatery, neither one could recognize anything on the menu. Leslie tried to explain to the waiter what the food looked like, so the waiter tried to bring them what he thought they ordered. Not even close. But the food was very good. Leslie asked the chief if he liked German food. The chief said, "Hell yes!" So the next day they found a German restaurant. They had jäger schnitzel, purple cabbage, spatzle with mushroom gravy, stewed kale, and German beer. For dessert they had orange-raspberry strudel. *Could life get any better?*

Leslie asked the other sailors if there was a real China, a China that was not as cosmopolitan as Shanghai. If there were smaller Chinese villages close, he wanted to see how the farmers and country people lived. They told him he would find that type of atmosphere up the Yangtze River, but the further up the river you went, the closer to the fighting you would get.

Leslie and Chief Joe McGhee welded at the American-British shipyards in Shanghai called the Kiangoan Dockyard and Engineering Works. They were to rebuild all the machine-gun emplacements on all the American ships in the harbor. He and the chief transferred from ship to ship, welding. The ships would sail up and down the coast for a week and then stay in port for a week. They put into Hong Kong for three days and again toured the city. The chief told Leslie that Hong Kong is just like England with just a few more Chinese. Hong Kong was an island city controlled by the British. Like Shanghai, it was a city of contrast. It had the very rich upper class and the poorest of the poor. Chief McGhee and Leslie toured the market area on the outskirts of the upper-class area and the slum areas. Leslie had to find a head (bathroom). He told the chief he had to sit down to do his business. They found a public building with heads.

Leslie walked in and declared, "I cannot do it here." The chief looked and saw it was one very large room with no interior walls or toilets. All it had were raised holes in the floor lined down each wall. Both men and women used it at the same time. Leslie said there was no way he could go in front of women. The chief said, : We go here or in our pants." Leslie was not pleased. He walked over to a hole, he pulled down his breaches and undershorts, and he squatted down. At about this time he saw a little hand reach through the hole and grab the roll of money out of his front pocket. He tried to grab the hand but could not for risk of falling on the nasty floor. He jerked up his pants, and he and the chief tried to find the hand that stole his money. To make it worse, he still had to go. They cursed all the way back to Shanghai, and of course, the chief just had to tell everybody about Leslie's event. In three days Leslie and the chief got orders to board the gunboat USS *Guam*. The *Guam* was a flat-bottomed riverboat. She had eight officers, fifty-five enlisted men, and sixteen coolies.

The Sino-Japanese broke out when the Japanese assaulted the Marco Polo Bridge. The Japanese headed toward Nanjing on the southern Yangtze River Delta. The Japanese army left a path of destruction and death in its path. They murdered helpless women and children. They committed countless rapes. When they took the city, they killed over three hundred thousand civilians and Chinese soldiers. Chiang Kai-shek's army collapsed. The American ambassador and his staff left Nanjing and went to Chung King 1,200 miles away on the USS *Luzon* gunboat. The American companies still wanted the United States military (China marines and China sailors) to protect their interest. The British and the Europeans put more boats and soldiers on the Yangtze River. Most of the fighting was taking place out in the country areas and way up in the deltas.

Leslie and other sailors talked about the war all the time. One of the marine officers boasted that the US Marines could whip the Japanese in a day. Leslie asked how.

"Well," said the officer, "the Japanese are very small and cannot see very well. It would be like fighting children." Some of the sailors actually believed that, but Leslie and the rest just laughed. They knew the Japanese had already captured Korea and vast parts of China. They were not childlike. They are a very good fighting force, well armed and well trained. Leslie knew the American China marines were very well trained and armed and could really fight. There were just not enough of them.

The gunboat USS *Guam* steamed up the Yangtze to a navy supply port on the river delta. A small marine company of the Fourth Marines billeted there. They were the security for American interest in the area. They were in the city of Dongting East, a medium-size city on the east banks of Dongting Lake, the largest freshwater in China. The lake was fed by four rivers. One of these was the Yangtze River. The city had about one hundred thousand people. The Italians and British keep a gunboat a piece in the lake area based out of Dongting city. Leslie and Joe McGhee had three days off and decided to tour this city. Due to the river flow and the mountains around part of it, the city smelled better than most of the places the men had been in China. The city was not near as modern as Shanghai nor as prosperous. They saw lots of military from many countries and a lot of civilian men but could not tell where they were from. Leslie heard German a lot but heard lots of other languages. They went to a town called Zigui, just outside of Dongting. They decided to eat and drink only Chinese food and beverages this time. They ate all kinds of vegetables fried in garlic and oil. It smelled and tasted very good. They had steaks called Yangtze dolphin and drank Chinese pinyin, which is a rice wine called yellow liquor. Chief Joe McGhee took Leslie to a bordello. Leslie had never really been in a bordello for himself or for the services they offered. McGhee ordered two women and a bottle of vodka for them. The women looked like skinny wet rats. They talked to the guys in a very fast pigeon English. They were taken to a room that had two twin beds and a curtain between them. They had two wash bowls and a dirty towel.

Leslie said, "I think I need a drink before I can do this."

Joe said, "No, this is for afterward."

It was not romantic or as much fun as it was with Maude, and he did not have to pay Maude.

As soon as he was finished, he started to dress when McGhee said, "Wait, wash it with the vodka. It will stop any disease you may catch."

Leslie, not being too experienced, did just that. It set him on fire. He hollered.

Joe said, "See, it's working."

Leslie started fanning himself. His prostitute starting laughing, "You Americans crazy."

Leslie and Joe drank what was left of the vodka and went to another slop shoot, a navy term for "bar," where you can also eat.

77

More pinyin and boiled crawfish and rice. The boys overate and way overdrank. They hired two rickshaws to carry them back to the boat. Halfway back, Leslie got sick. He fell out of the rickshaw and lost all the food and beverage he had consumed the last two hours. He then had the dry heaves. McGhee tried to help him when he got sick.

The rickshaw drivers took McGhee's watch and both men's roll of money.

The shore patrol (navy policeman) found the guys lying on the street passed out and took them to dock, where the ship was moored. They wished the guys good luck and laid them on the dock. Some of the Chinese coolies (porters) helped Leslie and Joe to their racks on the ship. The coolies had to keep an eye on the two to keep them safe so they could make it through the night.

That morning, Leslie woke up sick. His head hurt, his skin crawled, and he could not keep his breakfast down. One of the coolies took him to the engine room to the steam pipe area and sat him on the floor by the boiler. It was hot and steaming, very much like a steam room at a club. Leslie looked over, and there sat Joe, who was as sick as he was. Leslie sat by the wall for a spell and finally began to feel a little better. As he got better, he began to remember the last evening and all he had done. He began to cry because he realized he had cheated on Katie. He did not know what to do. He knew he would have to tell her. The coolie, named Chulee, brought him a mug of hot tomato soup with a paste in it called wasabi. It was extremely hot. The mixture cleared his head and his sinuses. The more he drank, the hotter it got and the better he felt. He looked at McGhee who was drinking the same thing. After an hour or two in the boiler room, Leslie came up to his rack, took a shower, and put on fresh work uniform called utilities. He now noticed he was moneyless. He knew he did not spend it all, so he wondered what happened to the twelve dollars he had. McGhee came in to the bay and asked Leslie if he knew what happened to his watch and money. Both men realized that they had been rolled. Leslie felt stupid and heartsick for what he had done and how he was robbed.

He could not think of anything good that he had done or fun. He did mark it down in his brain as a lesson he would not repeat.

One of his officers, Lieutenant Junior Grade MacConnel, asked him if he were all right and told him that he looked bad.

Leslie replied, "Lieutenant, may I ask you something in private?"

"Yes, Seaman, come up to the bow and let's talk."

"Lieutenant, I did something very stupid and I don't know what to do about it."

"Oh, tell me about it," said the lieutenant JG as he thought to himself, *Oh, I hope not this guy. He seems too much of a man. I might as well hear it.* Leslie told the lieutenant about his evening and about being with a prostitute and of being rolled somewhere.

The lieutenant said, "Is that all? I thought you were going to tell me you were a jeep."

"A what?"

"A jeep."

"What's that?"

"Don't worry about that now. What you did and what happened to you happens to most sailors on their first overseas duty. I'm not saying that it was the right thing to do, but it happens. Don't overreact. Take this as a lesson as to what not to do, especially if you have been drinking. Don't write your girl about a lack of judgment this far away from home. Now go back to work and get this off your mind."

Leslie felt a little better after his talk with the JG.

The *Guam* steamed back upriver. They were going to the last port at the head of the river 1,200 miles inland. The *Guam* was taking mail to the other gunboats, civilian passengers, new seamen, some ammunition, currency, and picking up mail going to the States, returning passengers, and seamen whose tours were finished. The trip would take about three weeks, a long voyage for a gunboat. The first gunboat the *Guam* met on the river at Wuhan was the USS *Asheville*. She is one of the larger boats with a crew of 150. They changed mailbags, put off three seamen and took on four, and resupplied the ammunition and the crews' pay and operating money in cash. Leslie found out that he was the only member of both crews from the *Guam* and the *Asheville* who was from Asheville.

The ships would meet in the middle of the river side by side, doing about eight to ten knots to keep pirates, Communists, or nationalist troops from firing on them. Further up the river they would have to contend with the Japanese army. The crews also would exchange war souvenirs, movies, and books (mostly trash books). When all the trading and resupplying was finished, the *Asheville* would slow and sail back to her base, and the *Guam* would head on up the river. Their next meeting with another gunship was off Chongqing. There they met the USS *Mindanao*. The *Mindanao* resupplied and paid and had only one sailor for the trip home. Three of the civilian passengers boarded the *Mindanao* and the crews traded again.

The *Guam* was about three hours up the river from Chongqing when she started taking fire—single shots, not automatic-weapon fire. Leslie had never been in conflict before. The captain called for battle stations. Leslie had trained so and the rest of the crew very smoothly went into battle ready. Leslie and his crew got their stretcher and went into their assigned passageway and knelt to one knee, ready. The shots were coming from a group of Chinese junks. The spotters on the *Guam* could not spot which junk the fire was coming from. There seemed to be twelve to fifteen shots per minute. The captain ordered the *Guam* to fire a three-inch shell in front of the junks but to be sure not to hit anything. *Boom*, the gun fired, and the shell hit about twenty yards in front of the lead junk. All of a sudden it seemed like all the junks opened fire on the *Guam*. Hundreds of bullets hit the *Guam*. The *Guam* steamed on upriver, away from the firing. The men on the junks started cheering. The captain ordered the crew to see if there was any damage to the ship and if anyone was hurt. The answer to both questions was no.

The captain made this announcement, "You can stand down, men. The threat is over. No one was hurt, and the ship received very minor damage. I'm proud of you guys. Our training proved to be very efficient. The crew did as it was asked with no one being injured. As we go further up the river, we will be getting closer to some of the conflicts, so keep your eyes open and be ready.

"Officers and warrant officers and chief petty officers, start wearing your side arms. Marines are to be armed at all times. Good luck, men."

The *Guam* steamed to a small city of about fifty thousand people on the river in the Sichuan province called Zigui. There they met the *Oahu* gunboat. As in the past meeting of other gunboats, they unloaded supplies and money, seamen and civilians. They boarded five civilians and five sailors. The *Oahu* needed their guns to have the armor plates welded in, so Leslie and McGhee were to stay with the *Oahu* and do the welding. Their captain told them he would be back to pick them up on the return voyage to Shanghai in about six to seven days and steamed away.

Leslie and McGhee welded all day and realized they had about a day's work left and they would be finished. McGhee told Leslie, "I've been talking to some of the guys on this ship, and they told me about a place where we could rent a couple of women for the evening, women not like what we had before but clean decent women. They also told me we could rent a couple of rooms while we're here instead of sleeping on a crowded ship. What do you think?"

"If we can eat French or German then I'm okay with that. Now I'm not going to sleep with anyone. I need to be loyal to Katie. Is that okay with you?"

"Sure, it will leave both women to me." The men put on their whites and headed to town. They hired a rickshaw driver and asked to be taken to the rent-a-woman place. The rickshaw driver told them they would have to change their money to Chinese money. They told the driver to take them to a bank to change their money. He told them of a better place to change money and that they would get more in exchange.

The boys said, "Sure." Leslie thought to himself, *This must be there Daddy Rabbit.* Leslie changed thirty-five dollars and McGhee changed twenty-eight dollars. The money changer gave them a black laundry bag to carry their new Chinese money. They had about a half a bushel full of money. The rickshaw driver took them to a hotel kind of place. They got two bedrooms with balconies and a sitting room. The bathroom was outside and down on the main floor in a building in the back. They had two big wide-mouth jugs in the room for peeing into. The maid emptied it two times a day. The room was ten pieces of Chinese money a day. The boys then had the rickshaw driver take them to the woman market to rent a couple of women. The rickshaw driver told them that he would be their driver there whole time in the city for only ten pieces of Chinese money a day; the boys agreed. He took them to the building where you could rent women. They went into the main room where the women were sitting. there were about twenty of them. The bar at one end was open. There were about fifty men sitting around. The women looked clean and intelligent. They had on old ragged clothes and no shoes. McGhee got them a couple of beers. The guys sat at a table to see what to do. They enjoyed watching the auction of women. They also watched chickens running in and out of the room with little boys trying to catch them. The men in the room were betting on who could catch a chicken and which chicken—or boys—got away. Leslie and Joe were having great fun. Leslie kept thinking how much like Franz he seemed to be. He wondered if Franz ever bet on a chicken or tried to buy a woman for the night. Knowing Franz, he probably did. McGhee started bidding on a lady, a smallish young, maybe sixteen—or seventeen-year-old girl who was very pretty. He would hold his finger up to bid.

Leslie asked, "What does the fingers mean?" McGhee replied, "I don't know. I watched the other men do it. Some won and some lost. I don't know if I'm winning or not, but it's fun. The bidding was over for the little girl, and everybody clapped. The old man who kept the women in place came over to McGhee and gave him the rope tied to the girls arm and spoke Chinese. Neither Leslie nor McGhee spoke the language, but it sounded different from the coolies on their ship. The old man held out his hand to McGhee. Leslie pulled out a handful of money and gave it to the old man.

The old man counted and stuck his hand out again. Leslie tried to act like he knew what he was doing and started handing the man one bill at a time. After the fifth bill, the old man cursed Leslie and stormed away.

McGhee asked, "What did he say?"

"I don't know, but I don't think he was happy. I think he said that he hoped your thing would drop off," replied Leslie. The girl sat with the men and drank out of McGhee's beer. She took a couple of bills out of the bag and went to the bar. She came back with another beer and a bowl of noodles. She slurped and sucked down the noodles like a starving dog.

Leslie said, "Let's go."

McGhee said, "No, let's get you one."

"No, I don't need one and I don't want one," answered Leslie, hanging his head down.

"Okay, let's finish our beers and see what else happens. This is fun."

Leslie agreed, and it was fun. About four women went through the auction. A young white Russian woman with short blondish hair was brought out.

McGhee's woman started talking to Leslie and motioning to the white Russian. She kept pulling his arm and talking very, very fast.

"I think she wants us to buy that one," said McGhee.

"Seems that way, don't it?" Leslie stuck his hand under his chin and wiggled his fingers. The auctioneer pointed at him. Other people were bidding also. The auctioneer looked at Leslie. He stuck his finger in his mouth and wiggled them. The auctioneer pointed at him again. Leslie and McGhee were laughing very hard at this. *The beer must be getting to me*, thought Leslie. He was having great fun. The girl at their table was pleading with them to bid. Leslie put his hand on his head and patted himself. The auctioneer looked at him again. Leslie stuck his index finger and acted like he was shooting himself. The auctioneer looked at him again and slapped his hand on the table. The old man led the white Russian over to the table again. Leslie handed him a large wad of money, and the old man cursed him, as he had to count it. The old man stuck out his hand again for more money. Leslie held out another hand full of money for the old man. The young Chinese girl grabbed Leslie's hand and started shouting at the old man. The old man cursed her and stormed away. The guys decided it was time to leave. They had what or who they had come for, and they had lots of fun doing it, but it was now time to go.

CHAPTER 11

WHITE RUSSIAN

Outside the building, their driver was waiting. McGhee told him to take them to either a German or a French restaurant, and it did not matter which one.

There driver asked, "Do you want a place where the woman can go in and eat?"

"Sure," said Leslie, and he asked, "Are there restaurants in China where Chinese are not allow to eat?"

"Yes, boss," replied the driver. "A lot of the European restaurants don't allow Chinese to go into them. But I was asking about the women, boss."

Leslie said, "Sure, let them eat with us. That's all I really want, not the chief. He does want more."

The driver and the Chinese girl had a conversation in Chinese. He then turned to Leslie and said, "Lechou (the girl's name) says she needs to have some clothes and a bath and so does the Russian girl."

"That's fine," replies Leslie. "How do we do that? And ask her the Russian's name."

"Boss, she say she don't know Russian name, and Russian don't speakie Chinese and Lechou don't speakie Russian. Neither speakie American. I'll take you to a store and to a bathhouse, okay?"

"Yes, that will be fine." Leslie motioned for the women to get into the rickshaw.

The driver waved his hand and said, "NO!" The women cowered away, looking down. Leslie asked Hojoh (the driver's name), "What are you doing?"

"Boss, rickshaw is for mens, not for womens. Womens have to follow behind the rickshaw. Now, boss, you and Boss McGhee get in. Womens will come behind us." Hojoh again spoke to the women and pointed down the road. The women started walking.

The boys loaded up and started out when McGhee asked the driver, "Hojoh, when did the Chinese invent the rickshaw? How many hundreds of years old are they?"

"Boss McGhee, rickshaw been in China about fifty years old. Rickshaw now in Korea, Japan. Rickshaw came from America, invented in New York."

"Are you sure?"

"Yes, boss."

McGhee asked Leslie, "Did you know that?"

Leslie said, "No, I've never seen one before I got to China." They arrived at a store of some sort, and Hojoh told Leslie to give the girl some money, which Leslie did. While the girls shopped and took a bath, the driver took the boys to a cockfight. Neither of the men had been to a fight before.

McGhee said, "This is a lot of excitement over a bird." Leslie agreed. Hojoh showed the boys how to bet and how to pick a bird.

"Let me have monies, boss. You watch me and learn. It's easy," said Hojoh.

The boys killed about an hour at the fights. Hojoh told them they had won and gave them both a couple of bills. He stuck a large wad of bills in his pocket. The group went back to the store where they had left the women.

Leslie asked, "Are we sure they are going to be there? Want they run away."

"No, boss, they have nowhere to go. They not from here. They from up north." And sure enough when they got to the store, there were the women, clean and dressed better in Chinese sandals, black silk pants, very colorful long shirts, and straw coolie hats. The ladies also smelled of jasmine.

"Okay," said Leslie, "now let's get some chow, German or French." The guys sat in their rickshaw again, and off they went. They traveled in a big circle in places most white men can't go into. They saw nationalist flags and Communist flags. They finally came to a little restaurant setting in a small bay that was just beautiful. It had statues of Chinese gods and water fountains and lots of flowers growing everywhere. Hojoh told them that this was a local French restaurant and that the women could go in and eat with them. Hojoh turned to Lechou and gave her a bunch of stern orders. He turned to the guys and said, "I've told Lechou to order for you and to take care of you while you eat. Boss, I need a little money to make repairs to the rickshaw. I can repair it while you eat." He held out his hand.

Leslie gave him the bag of money, and Hojoh picked out the money he needed. He told them he would be outside when they finished eating. Lechou led them all into the restaurant.

McGhee said to Leslie, "Did you notice we're the only white men in here?"

"Yeah, I can see that. Just smile and be nice. Do you have your hawkbill on you?"

"I sure do. How about you?"

"I never go anywhere without it." It was something Daddy Rabbit had taught him.

Daddy Rabbit told him to carry two knives. You always pull out the first knife with your off hand and kind of fumble with it in your hand and drop it. The man you're going to fight will always pick it up to cut you with your own knife. While he's picking it up, you take your hawkbill out with your good hand and cut him to pieces. It works every time.

Lechou found them a table by the window overlooking a bird bath with statues of turtles and lizards on it. When the waiter came over and spoke to them, Lechou spoke to him. She ordered and bowed to him and he left. The waiter came out carrying hot tea and some kind of fruit mixed with grapes, lychees, and orange slices. As Leslie ate the fruit, he would motion to each bite and then to Lechou. She would in turn say the Chinese name, or at least Leslie thought she was giving it the Chinese name.

She could have been saying, "That is poison, stupid American, eat up." The next course was a large fish steak, very good and very hot and spicy. Leslie pointed to it and

Lechou said in Chinese, "Paddlefish." Then came a fried stalk of lettuce. Leslie pointed and Lechou said, "Bok

Choy." The last course was a thick chicken broth. The waiter then brought out a bottle of rice beer. It had a peculiar taste but was good. McGhee ask if Leslie thought it was French or German. Lechou took money from the bag and paid the waiter, who smiled very big and bowed very deep. Leslie thought to himself, *The way he acted, we must have tipped him well.* When they got outside there was Hojoh waiting for them.

Leslie asked him, "What kind of restaurant was this? German of French?"

"Boss, that be French restaurant." Leslie and McGhee laughed. Leslie asked Hojoh, "What does a paddlefish look like?"

"If you want me to, I'll show you one on way back to hotel, boss."

"Okay," said Leslie, "let's go."

On the way back, Hojoh took them to the docks. He spoke to many fishermen, and then he motioned for the group to follow him. They got to a dock where many men were in the process of rolling an enormous fish on to the deck.

Hojoh pointed to it and said, "That a paddlefish."

Leslie said, "That's the biggest fish I've ever seen. It must be twelve to fifteen feet long and weigh five hundred pounds, damn."

"Damn!" said McGhee. (The paddlefish can grow to twenty feet and weigh up to one thousand pounds. It looks similar to a swordfish but has a much thicker sword and is much, much uglier. They are freshwater fish that mainly live in the rivers of Asia.)

Hojoh said, "That good fish. It feed many families. Always good luck to catch."

When they got to the hotel, Leslie told Hojoh to tell the Russian, "Thank you, had a nice time."

"Boss, where she go? She have no money and she have no place to go."

"Here, give her money for a room." Leslie gave Hojoh a wad of bills.

Hojoh said, "Wait here, boss. I go get her a room." When Hojoh came out of the hotel, he had rolled the bills into a nice little roll, and he said, "No can stay here, boss. No woman without man." He gave the roll back to Leslie. Leslie could not tell, but the money felt half the weight it was before.

"What am I supposed to do?" asked Leslie.

"Girl have to stay in your room, boss, or she be arrested or even killed by bad people."

"Okay, okay," said Leslie, "tell them to go to the room. I need to go to the head."

McGhee said, "Me too."

When the boys got to the room, they found that the oil lamps were low and the windows were open. There was a girl in each room or, I should say, in each bed.

McGhee said, "I'll see you in the morning."

Leslie said, "No, wait. What am I supposed to do with her?"

"Don't know, don't care. I have a job to do in that room and I'm late. She may start without me." He went into his room and closed the door.

Leslie said to himself, *Where am I suppose to sleep?* He looked around, and the only place to sleep was on the floor or in the chair or in the bed in the other room with the Russian. Hell, he paid for the bed, he paid for the room, he paid for the chow—and it was very good too—and he paid for the girl. Hell, he was going to sleep in the bed. She would have to sleep in the corner of the bed. Leslie went in to his room and undressed down to his Skivvies (boxer shorts and T-shirt). He turned down the lamp and got in bed. The

Russian had all the covers on herself, so Leslie pulled them on to himself. After all, he was paying for them. As soon as he pulled the covers, he saw she was naked and trying to cover herself with her hands. He immediately threw some of the cover on her, but it was too late. He had seen her nakedness, and it stirred him. His body started to react to his thoughts when she slid over to him. He thought to himself, *I'll just mess around a bit but not really do anything.* And he started kissing his little white Russian. Leslie woke up hearing McGhee calling his name.

Leslie answered, "Okay, I hear you. What do you want?"

"We got to go to work, big boy. Come on."

"Oh yeah, I forgot. Give me a minute."

He looked over and saw the Russian and remembered his evening with her, and he started getting aroused again. He quickly got dressed and went downstairs and was surprised to see McGhee sitting in Hojoh's rickshaw, ready to go.

"Morning."

"Morning."

"And good morning, bosses," said Hojoh. Leslie got into the rickshaw, and off they went to work on the USS *Oahu* at the docks. McGhee asked, "Leslie, how was your evening?"

"I don't want to talk about it, but it was one of the better evenings of my life," he said as he thought to himself, *Boy I'm glad Maude taught me some of, or really all of, that stuff.* Hojoh asked them if they wanted him to wait till lunch and get them some local foods.

"No," said McGhee, "we'll eat here on the boat. We should be through about fifteen hundred hours (3:00 p.m.). Pick us up then."

"Okay, boss." He stuck out his hand. McGhee looked at Leslie, and Leslie pulled out a wad of bills and told Hojoh to take what was need. Hojoh counted out some bills slowly, making sure that Boss Leslie watched. Hojoh left the rickshaw on the dock and walked away. The boys started to weld. They were able to do two .50-caliber machine guns by lunch.

They had lettuce and tomato and cheese sandwiches with an apple. Leslie grabbed a second sandwich, which was sardines, lettuce, and tomato. He said to McGhee, but also wanted the other dozen or so sailors in the mess hall to hear him, "Chief, isn't the lettuce called bok choy?"

McGhee looked at it and said, "You know, I believe so." The boys laughed. When they were finished eating they went down on the dock and started messing with the rickshaw. One of them would sit on it while the other pulled it. Other sailors came down and wanted a ride or to pull it. Everybody was getting a turn, and the horsing around started getting rough when one sailor turned it too close to the edge with three sailors on it and the wheel broke and the whole rickshaw fell into the Yangtze River.

Everybody laughed, but Leslie said, "Guys, we are going to have to pay for this. Now pass the hat." Each of the men involved kicked in a few bucks. Leslie counted the money, and he had fifteen dollars, five of which was his. They went back to work and welded armor on a .30-caliber machine gun. They changed from there utilities to their white uniforms and headed down to the dock to wait for Hojoh.

Hojoh came walking down the dock and waved at the guys and started looking for his rickshaw. Leslie went to Hojoh and told him what had happened to the rickshaw. He said they were very sorry and would pay for a new one. He gave Hojoh the money he collected and asked Hojoh if that were enough. Hojoh said, "No, boss, not for a good one."

Leslie said, "Take some of this Chinese money to pay for it also."

"Okay, thanks, boss"

"Now let's find a way to the hotel."

Hojoh said, "Let me do it, boss."

"Okay."

Hojoh left. In about ten minutes, he came back riding in a single-man rickshaw, and another coolie was pulling an empty two-man rickshaw. The boys got into the two-man rickshaw and off they went. When they got to the hotel,

Leslie asked Hojoh, "Hojoh, are you buying one of these rickshaws?"

"No, Boss Leslie, these are my brothers'. Rickshaws belong to them. I buy one tomorrow morning. Brothers work for us tonight. Where we go tonight, boss?"

"If we had French last night then let's have German or Italian tonight," replied Leslie. McGhee and Leslie went to their room to pick up their dates. The ladies had on more new clothes and looked and smelled great. Hojoh told Lechou the name of the restaurant and how to get there. The ladies started walking, and the men got into the rickshaws and headed there themselves. They got to a mud-block building with flowering vines hanging on it. It had two big rock ponds with big koi fish in them.

"I wonder what kind of restaurant this is?" asked McGhee.

"Don't know," replied Leslie, "but it sure smells good."

Lechou led them to a table overlooking the ponds. She ordered them rice beers to start, and then the meal came out. They had a big bowl of a kind of sticky rice, chopped vegetables that were fried in a clear sauce, a baked chicken with the head still on it, a platter of fried chicken feet, and sliced water chestnuts fried in pig fat. This was another great meal, if you didn't have to look at the chicken head. The two women seemed to really like the chicken feet. After they ate the meat off of the feet, they would pick on the toes with toenails on them with their teeth. The boys would not do that. When the meal was finished, Lechou took the money roll from Leslie and paid the bill. The group went outside to find Hojoh. He was waiting right there and he said, "Boss, I have something special for you." The group with Hojoh walked across the street, and out on a dock, there was a small sampan boat with two oarsmen in it and a helmsman.

Hojoh said, "Get in, bosses. This is my cousin's sampan, and he is going to take you mens and your womans on a ride through the delta. Lots of animals and birds and fish in the delta areas. Boss, let me see the money roll to pay him and his men." Leslie gave him the money roll, and Hojoh unrolled a lot of bills to pay his cousins. He gave what was left back to Leslie. Leslie figured they had already spent about 10 percent of their money. With four days left to go before there ship picks them up, they should be okay with money. They all got into the sampan and sat down on little benches. There was not room for Hojoh, so he told them he would see them when his cousins brought them back to the dock. The trip was very interesting. It was quiet and very beautiful. Leslie sat with his girl in his arms and he felt great. His life could not get any better than this. Hojoh's cousins would point out all kinds of exotic animals and birds and reptiles. The flowers were spectacular. They saw and picked orchids, lotuses, Poneys, giant buttercups, lilies, poppies, and pomegranates. The smell in the sampan was overpowering. It was so nice. Their trip took about two hours. It was almost 2000 hours (8:00 p.m.). Hojoh was waiting at the dock with the two rickshaws. Leslie grabbed the front of the rickshaw and motioned for the ladies to get in, which they sheepishly did. Leslie started down the street with the rickshaw.

McGhee jumped into the other rickshaw and hollered, "Follow him."

Hojoh told the other driver to follow Boss Leslie. Hojoh and his brother took off after Leslie. It did not take them a minute to catch him. The ladies and Leslie were laughing and having a good time. Leslie would not stop pulling the rickshaw. Hojoh and his brother were begging him to stop.

McGhee kept asking, "Do you want to race? I'll bet you a day's pay we can get to the hotel before you." Both sailors hopped and hollered. They were having a great time. They finally got to the hotel. Hojoh's brothers were raising hell. Leslie rolled off a couple of bills to give to Hojoh to pass on to his brothers. This seemed to calm them down a bit.

The ladies took the boys to the bathhouse. Lechou said something to the old woman who seemed to run the place. She motioned for the group to come behind a paper wall with large beautiful birds painted on it. In that area was a very large wooden tub full of hot scented water. The old woman left, and the girls started taking the guys' clothes off and motioned the boys into the water. The guys sat on little stools in the water that came up to the middle of their chest. At about this time, the old woman brought a tray with white rice wine and little cookies on it. Lechou took the tray and sat it on a shelf that hung over the tub. The ladies took off their clothing and also got into the tub. Lechou called to the old woman, and she came over with a large pitcher of hot water and poured it into the tub. The water in the tub immediately got hotter. The women poured the boys wine and started sponging them off. The rough sponges and the hot water felt pretty good. The boys, being boys, started splashing each other and then started wrestling. The women started scolding them, but the boys did not understand any of the words. They just laughed. After the bath, the group went to their rooms and made love.

Leslie again said to himself, *Could life get any better?*

The following morning, the boys had to get up and go to work. On the gunboat they finished up the rest of the welding. Now they have three days off and no work to do. At noon they left the boat and met Hojoh on the dock with his new two-man rickshaw. Hojoh took them to the hotel. The women were waiting in the garden of the hotel for them. Lechou went over to Hojoh and had a conversation with him in Chinese. He came over to Leslie and said, "Boss, she (pointing with his thumb at Lechou) want to go to a market to buys food to cooks for you, okay?" The white Russian went over to Leslie and touched his face and rubbed it. She laughed and said something in Russian and laughed again. Neither Leslie nor McGhee had shaven in three days, and they had a good stubble started. (The China sailors were not required to shave, and most did not, except the officers.) Leslie grabbed her hand and kissed it.

Leslie had replenished their money supply at the gunboat. Two days ago on the gunboat, Leslie had emptied out the bag of Chinese money and separated them by color. He had made twenty stacks and rolled them into very large rolls. He put two rolls in his pockets and one into McGhee's pocket. The rest he locked in his locker on board.

The boys had spent three rolls of money so far, so they got two more rolls apiece this time.

The group headed to the market. It was an open-air market that led to different buildings. It seemed to be the central market for the town. It was crowded with Chinese civilians, Chinese army (national and Communist), and Europeans and Americans (civilians and military). The market had every kind of small animal, birds, and reptiles in cages or pens of some sort. They had about every bird or fowl dead and hanging by their feet, fish on lines hanging, and big baskets of fruits and vegetables. Some they recognized; most they did not know. They kept asking Hojoh what each was. They had asked so many times that he told Lechou to start naming each as they got to it. They could not understand her but did learn a name or two. They went into a building that had every kind of dried bug, small fish, and reptiles in large jars. Lechou reached into a jar and pulled out a handful of dried fish. They were small like sardines but were yellow in color. She gave one to each of them to try. The four of them tried it. Leslie thought it was salty and fishy but quite good.

McGhee called the group over to him, told them to look, and pointed to a shelf of jars with dried animal penises. Leslie grabbed himself in the crouch and moaned; the group started laughing. Next, Lechou had them try a tiny dried squid; it also was good. Lechou would buy an item, Leslie paid for it, and then the Russian would carry each of the packages. They came to a melon table. It had melons the boys had never seen before. They got to taste each one. Some were sweet and very good, and some were sweet but tasted bad. They came to a grill with chicken feet on it. The girls each got one. Leslie and McGhee declined. They came to the fish tables—again lots of fish that they did not recognize. On the table was the biggest catfish Leslie had ever seen. It had to be three hundred pounds. He could have stuck his whole head in its mouth. There were all kinds of very large shrimp and mussels. The shopping trip took about two hours. The Russian had her hands full and Lechou helped her. The men were not allowed to carry anything. They went to the gardens at the hotel and found a place to cook. It had a stone oven with a round hole in the middle. The top of the stove looked like a big rock pot with a hole in the middle. The women built a fire in the oven and put a metal pot on top. The pot looked like an upside-down coolie hat. The girls kept calling it a wok. They added oil and spices and began to fry the shrimp and mussels. They had put a pot of rice in the front opening of the stove. They had purchased a large green leaf filled with a very strong-smelling brown paste. When the rice was finished, Lechou put the paste on top of the rice. The hot steam of the rice kind of melted the brown paste, and it started smelling less strong and kind of nice. As soon as the shrimp and mussels were finished, Lechou put the vegetables in the pot and turned and stirred the vegetables until they were also done. Lechou put little black seeds and garlic in the vegetables. *Whoa,* thought Leslie, *this food is great.* Leslie had never had shrimp with the heads and legs on them. He peeled his shrimp and ate only the tails. He noticed the women ate the heads and the unpeeled tails. His Russian also ate Leslie's shrimp heads. The boys drank rice beer and the ladies had hot tea. Leslie thought to himself, *Can life get any better that this?* The girls gave the men there baths again and they had a great night. Leslie and McGhee woke up and felt their beards. McGhee being light haired so was his beard stubble, it need many more day of growth before in looked decent. Leslie's hair was brown and so was his beard. It was already looking pretty good. The boys told Hojoh that they wanted to go fishing in the river. Hojoh told the boys the best fishing spot was up in the smaller creeks and streams on the other side of the river. The river at this point was a quarter mile across. The group, both couples and Hojoh, headed to Hojoh's cousin's sampan to take their fishing trip. The girls had packed their lunch. It consisted of fried chicken feet, fried chicken wings, fried chicken necks, rice wrapped in a big leaf, and lychees. Of course they brought plenty of rice beer. Hojoh baited their poles for them, and they laid back in the sampan to do some fishing and daydreaming. Leslie started thinking about Katie. He was seeing her face on the Russian. He thought he could smell Katie. He really wanted to hold her. He really needed to go home. He decided he would try in about six months. He started feeling better when a couple of bullets hit the boat. The group lay down and tried to get as low as possible in the boat, and again—*bang, bang*—bullets hit the boat. Hojoh's cousin steered the boat into the marsh. They got behind some tall grasses and hid. Hojoh said, "Boss Leslie, Boss McGhee, we stay here a while till Communist leave. They never stay long. They come this close for food and recruits, maybe kill some nationalist soldiers."

The current took them further downstream, and they decided to let that happen. The further away from the shooting, the better. A few more hundred feet down the river they floated to a clump of bamboo. The bamboo grove was about a quarter mile long and across. Hojoh said, "We safe here, boss. Communist can't go through bamboo. They sat for a while, and then Lechou started to unpack the food and make a picnic for them. They had nothing they could do but eat. Leslie tried the chicken neck. *Not bad*, he thought. He really liked the wings. Lechou had put a tiny little red pepper with them. It was hotter than hot but had a good flavor. He finally decided to try the feet. It was like chewing leather off of a stick. It tasted fine. It was just a lot of work. He also could not pick his teeth with the toes or toenails. They kept drifting down the river. They finally decided that they were far enough away that they were out of range of the Communists. Now they had to worry about pirates. The river was full of them. They saw a British gunboat steaming up the river. They started waving and hailing the gunboat. His Majesty's Ship, *Leicester*, sounded their horn to let the sampan know they saw them. The sampan rowed out to the gunboat and asked for a tow up the river for about ten miles. McGhee told the British who they were and that they were fired upon by the Communists. The gunboat tossed them a line to tow them back upstream. Leslie and McGhee went aboard *Leicester*. They were questioned by the officers and had a beer with the British welders. It took the gunboat about thirty minutes to tow them where they wanted and bid them good-bye.

Leslie told McGhee, "We need to check in at our gunboat and find out if they are looking for us or if they need anything fixed because of the Communist attack."

"Good idea," said McGhee. Leslie told Hojoh to take the women back to the hotel and then to pick him and McGhee up at their ship.

Hojoh replied, "No, boss. Womans don't ride, I'll take you and Boss McGhee to boat. Womans can walk to hotel."

Leslie knew he could do nothing about the Chinese requiring women to walk. He just shrugged his shoulders, and he and McGhee got on the rickshaw, and Hojoh took them to the docks. The captain of the gunboat wanted armor plates put on each side of the wheelhouse and wanted it now. The boys took about three hours to do the job. The boys were told that their ship would pick them up at 8:30 a.m. the day after tomorrow, so they have to be ready. The ship was only going to slow down, and they had to row out to board her.

Leslie and McGhee had Hojoh take them to the hotel. They spent the rest of the afternoon packing all the stuff and souvenirs they had bought. Leslie had gifts for all his family members. He also had to bid his Russian good-bye. He did not know exactly how to tell her since they did not speak each other's language, but he would think of something. Leslie told Hojoh to take them to a new restaurant that they had not been to.

"Yes, Boss Leslie. I know the place for you." Leslie and McGhee bathed and put on fresh whites and off they went. On the way to the restaurant, Leslie had Hojoh pull over in front of a flower vendor. He bought both girls a large bouquet of beautiful great-smelling flowers in bamboo flowerpots. The flowerpots were about eighteen inches tall and four inches across and had dragons carved on them. The base was set in an iron ring that made the bottom heavy and hard to turn over. The girls seemed to love their flowers. They came to a restaurant that was a mud-brick and bamboo building. It smelled good. Again, Lechou ordered for everyone. They had fish with fish eggs and sliced oranges wrapped in leaves. They had chopped pork and pork fat with corn wrapped in corn flour wrapped in corn husk and baked. Their vegetables came in a thick broth that had both a sweet and a sour taste (very good). The boys drank rice beer and the ladies had hot tea. Leslie paid Lechou, and Lechou paid for the food. On the way back to the hotel, Leslie asked Hojoh to come to the room and explain some things to the girls.

"Yes, boss, I will do it." In the hotel room, Leslie asked Hojoh to translate and Hojoh agreed. Leslie started, "Ladies, McGhee and I really appreciate your spending this time with us. We feel so glad that you were able to make this much time for us. We will always remember you when we think about China. Tonight is our last night together and we wish you well."

Hojoh spoke to the ladies. He then turned to Leslie and said, "Boss, where do womans go? Where do womans live and how?"

"I don't know," replied Leslie. "They need to go back to where they came from."

"No no, boss, womans belong to you. You buy at market. They have no place to go back to. Nobody, nowhere Russian from, and she don't know where she is now. The womans go on ship with you."

"No no," said Leslie.

"What do you mean these women belong to us? That we bought them? It's illegal to buy and sell people."

"No, boss. This China. You cans buy womans. Womans like goat. You buy and trade anytime."

McGhee finally jumped into the conversation and said, "You can't bring a woman on an American warship to live. Now just tell these girls to just away."

"Where they go, Boss McGhee? Nobody want woman who sleep with white man. They lower class, will probably be killed."

McGhee turned to Leslie and asked what they were going to do.

Leslie said, "I don't know. We need to sleep on it, and we need to hope we have an idea in the morning." As Leslie was getting ready for bed, he kept thinking, *I wish I could talk to my mom about this. She's smart, and she would know what to do.* Leslie had another great night, but his thoughts were, *She, the Russian, doesn't have a clue as to what's happening in her life. She just does what she is told to do or motioned to do. What the hell kind of life is that?*

That morning Leslie yelled down to Hojoh to come up to the room. He had an idea. Leslie had everyone sit down to hear his idea. He asked Hojoh to find a home for sale he could afford and that was safe for the girls. Leslie motioned to his stomach and his mouth to show Lechou that he was hungry. She nodded her head that she understood. She took the Russian with her to the garden where the kitchen was. McGhee and Leslie got dressed and packed up all their stuff and all the souvenirs they had bought. They could not believe all the stuff they had. Lechou called for them to come to the garden to eat. She had made egg roll, which were eggs, ham, beans, onions, and a thick sauce wrapped in a thin sheet of dough. They were great. She had also sliced some mangoes that were ripe and cold. Hojoh came back and told Leslie that he had found the perfect house for the girls.

CHAPTER 12

HOME SWEET HOME

The group followed him to a rock and mud-brick home. It was three rooms, two bedrooms, and a large kitchen/eating room. There was a small garden and fountain in the back. It was clean and did not smell bad. Leslie asked Hojoh to tell the girls it's for them and ask if they liked it. Lechou clapped her hands and used her words and sign language to tell the Russian.

Leslie said, "Well, it's settled then. Hojoh, tell the owner we'll take it." At that time, Leslie held out the rolls of money. Hojoh took five rolls and left. In about ten minutes, Hojoh came into the house with a rolled-up piece of paper. He gave it to Lechou to examine, and she seemed very happy and hugged Leslie. Then the Russian hugged Leslie, and then McGhee hugged Leslie, and all of them started laughing.

Leslie said, "We need to go to the market and buy some food and other stuff for the house." As the group headed out of the house, Leslie noticed Hojoh's brother at the house next door.

Leslie asked, "Hojoh, is that your brother? Does he live beside the girls?"

"Yes, boss," replied Hojoh.

"Hojoh, where do you live?" Hojoh pointed to the house across the path. Now Leslie understood. Hojoh had sold them one of his family's houses. It did not matter as long as the girls were safe. He figured he had just overpaid for the home.

The group headed to the market arm in arm, the four of them abreast. Hojoh followed, pulling the rickshaw. They first went to the food market, and the girls bought all kinds of dried food and spices. Next they purchased two big tin tubs and all kinds of tools—hammer, rake, hoe, shovel, wire, string. They bought bed linens and things like that. Lechou wanted a set of the pots called woks. They got plates, bowls, and cooking utensils. They piled the rickshaw full, and McGhee added three oil lamps and a gallon of oil. The group went back to the house and started setting up. As the group unpacked and arranged everything, the Russian had taken a tub into one of the bedrooms and was filling it with warm water. She went into the main room and got Leslie by the hand and took him to the tub. She took off all his clothes and had him stand in the tub, where she used a rough sponge to scrub him down. He felt alive and aroused and he felt good. The Russian gave him a man's Chinese robe to put on. He went into the main room where Lechou had prepared the evening meal. She had egg rolls again, this time with chicken or fish instead of ham. The sauce was much spicier, and she had a sliced pineapple that was very ripe and sweet. It was the first time Leslie had seen a real pineapple. He had only seen them sliced and in cans. He noticed the Russian was filling the tub with warm water again. After the meal, the Russian took Leslie by the hand and took him into the bedroom again. She undressed and stood in the tub. Leslie knew what to do, and he started giving her a bath. *Wow, what a night. Life could not get any better than this.* Early the next morning, Leslie and McGhee put on fresh cleaned whites. The girls had washed and ironed them during the night. They called Hojoh from across the path.

"Hojoh, tell Lechou to take the rest of the money, about four rolls, and to live on until I get back. It may be a while, I don't know." Leslie figured the money could last a year. "Now take us to the dock." The boys hugged the girls and all had a tearful good-bye.

Leslie and McGhee signed back on to the ship. They were told to get into the motor launch and that the *Guam* was headed their way. The motor launch met the *Guam* in the middle of the river with mail, some supplies, a couple of civilians, and its two welders. The boys boarded the *Guam* and it picked up steam and headed down the river. Leslie and McGhee kept the crew occupied with their stories of the slave market, the Communist attack, and the foods. Leslie kept thinking to himself, *I wonder if I could take these recipes back to Asheville and have a Chinese restaurant. I'll bet that Franz would think it was a great idea.*

The captain called the boys up in his dayroom. "Gentlemen, did you see any American officer with the Communist soldiers?"

"No, sir, I don't think I even saw an American with the Communist soldiers," replied Leslie.

"Nor me," said McGhee.

"I thought you said you were attacked by the Communists," said the captain.

"We were, Captain, but we had to hide in the bottom of a sampan since we were not armed and we had women with us," said Leslie. "We saw a lot of nationalist troops, American and British troops, sir."

"Sir," asked Leslie, "which side are we on? The Communist or the nationalist?"

"I think we are on both sides right now. We're on whoever is fighting the Japanese side," replied the captain. "This is all unofficial. We were completely neutral until the Japanese sank the USS *Panay* and a couple Standard Oil tankers. The Japanese paid us for the ships, but a lot of good men, American sailors, died that day, so we want the Chinese to beat the hell out of them. Now that's unofficial and off the record."

"Thank you, sir," said Leslie and McGhee. The boys had a new list of things that had to be welded on the *Guam*. They also had some bullet holes to weld over.

McGhee said, "It looks like they also had some action. There must be a hundred holes on this side. If you look down on the side of the hull, you see where another hundred bounced off. With the Chinese shooting at us and us not liking the Japanese and the Communists fighting the nationalist, who are we suppose to shoot at?"

"I think we're just supposed to duck at all times," replied Leslie. When Leslie went to bed, he had dreams of his Russian with Katie's face. His Russian was the first woman he had ever seen her breastatis, he had seen her naked. With Maude it was always in the dark and they never got undressed. He woke up in a sweat. He hopped up and went up on deck where he could get some cool fresh air and relieve himself. He went back to his rack and wrote Katie a letter. He wanted to see her. It took another two weeks before they docked in Shanghai, their home port. Leslie was reassigned to the *Asheville* and partnered back up with Gay Woody, the fireman from basic. Gay had shipped out thirty days after Leslie and signed on the *Asheville*. Each had great stories to tell. The *Asheville* coast hopped down the China and Vietnam coast. They stopped in Hong Kong, Hanoi, and Saigon. Leslie tried to buy souvenirs symbolizing each country. Leslie was proud of himself for not getting seasick any more, even in choppy water. He had a lot of work to do on the *Asheville*, saltwater really made these ships rust fast. They had to be scraped and painted at all times. Leslie had to cut out some rusty spots and weld over them. The cities were beautiful, each with a different European influence. Saigon was very much French, Hanoi was also French with a little Dutch, Hong Kong was like being in London, Shanghai was a mixture of German, French, but mostly British. This cruise took three weeks and Leslie was glad to be back in Shanghai. The first thing Leslie did after he signed back on the *Guam* was to look up McGhee. McGhee was onshore welding at the shipyard. Leslie helped him finish his job for the day, and they took off for a good dinner and some beers. They went down on Canal Street, where the German restaurant and beer gardens were located. It's name was Schnitzel Haus, and that's what the boys wanted, jäger schnitzel and dark German beer. They were tired of rice beer (gives one gas). They met some sailors from the *Asheville* and some of their shipmates. Three of the sailors could sing German beer songs, including Leslie. Leslie could sing the songs in German. As the group drank more, they sang louder. A large group of Italian sailors were drinking and eating in the garden next to the Americans. One of the Italians screamed to shut up to the Americans and threw an empty beer mug over the hedge, about four of the Americans threw four empty mugs back over the hedge on the Italians. Next, the Italians threw food and empty beer bottles over at the Americans. The Americans started climbing over the hedge and a big all-out fight took place. Food, chairs, beer bottles, plants, and sailors were thrown everywhere. The shore patrol and the fleet marines came in with batons swinging. The shore patrol arrested nine American sailors and eleven Italian sailors. No one got away. The duty officer at the brig called the *Asheville* and The *Guam* XOs to come and get their men. Each ship's XO came and got their men. The XO of the *Guam* lined his four men up and chewed them up and spit them out. He said, "You are a disgrace to the flag, to the navy, and to the *Guam*." Their uniforms were ripped up and they looked like hell. The men were beginning to sober up and they felt like hell too. "You men are going to spit shine the four heads on the ship. The four of you have KP (kitchen patrol—to wash all the dishes, scrub the entire galley, and serve the food). This will let the coolies off for a day. Now get back to the ship. SSS (shit, shower, shave) and put on clean utilities and start the work detail." The four men got into the back of an open truck and headed to the ship. The XO leaned back to Leslie and asked, "What was this fight about? I'm going to have to tell the old man (the captain of the ship)."

"It was just a sailor's fight, sir."

"Oh, who has the biggest anchor? Was that it, Sailor?"

Leslie laughed. "Yes, sir." Leslie had to start his beard over when he was assigned to the *Asheville*. He had to shave. Only China sailors were allowed to grow facial hair. McGhee's beard still looked ragged.

The crew got the news that they were to lead three tankers up the Yangtze and then escort a cargo ship back to Shanghai and then escort another cargo ship up to where they had left the tankers. The tankers would now be full of crude oil, and the *Guam* had to escort them back to Shanghai. When they took the first cargo up the river, they were to take half of a marine company, about fifty men and their equipment, to where they had left the tankers and pick up another cargo ship. On their return trip back upriver with the other cargo ship, they were to bring the rest of the marine rifle company, another fifty men and their equipment, and reconnect with the tankers and bring them back to Shanghai. Each trip up and back for them would only take five days. Other gunship would take the tankers the rest of the way upriver, where the USS *Luzon* would be waiting for them. The whole cruise would take about three weeks. The USS *Tutuila* would follow the tankers up the river and follow them down the whole way. Standard Oil did not want to lose any more tankers. They had to contend with pirates, the Japanese, and the Chinese nationalist army.

The first trip up the river and back went very smoothly. On the second trip up escorting the cargo ship and carrying marines, they ran into bandits or pirates or nationalists or all three. At this time in history in China, one was never sure who the other side really was. The US Navy tried to do its job without killing anyone, but sometimes it could not be helped. On this trip, a large group of sampans, maybe twenty, and three junks (larger Chinese ships) blocked the river to try to stop the *Guam* and the cargo ship. The *Guam* and the cargo ship had just rounded a large curve in the river in the Hunan province at the town of Hung Ho. The captain of the *Guam* ordered his men to hook up fire hoses and steam hoses. He reminded the crew not to kill anyone. The marines wanted to fight; they were all armed. The captain had to order the marines to go into the cabins and not to come out unless asked for. The marines did not like this but slowly complied to orders. The captain thought to himself, *If I need the* Dogs of War *I know where you're at.* The pirates tried to block the ships, but the ships were too big and going too fast, about ten knots. The American sailors would spray a jet of water on the sampan and turn some of them over. If a pirate tried to board, they would be sprayed with steam. A junk started to head toward the bow of the gunboat when the captain ordered the *Guam* to fire a three-inch shell over her bow. *Boom*, the gun roared. The shell went over the bow of the junk and exploded in the water. That was all they had to see, and it turned to give the gunboat and her cargo ship a wide berth. When the *Guam* stopped and the cargo ship docked, the marines unloaded their equipment and their men. Just before the *Guam* made contact with the other cargo ship going to Shanghai, they started being shot at from the left side of the river. That area was supposed to be under nationalist control. The captain ordered his men to get armed and stay down. "Don't make yourself a target. Get down."

The XO asked, "Captain, should we return fire?"

"No, we don't know who is firing at us. We may hit civilians," replied the captain. "We'll be out of range soon."

The marines, who had just gotten to shore, started yelling at the shooters, "Come on and shoot at us! Why don't you shoot at us? You shoot at us and we'll come and kill you!" They were all standing on the riverbank, yelling and waving. The XO said, "Those guys are crazy."

"Who?" said the captain.

"Those China marines. They're crazy."

The captain said, "Stand down, we're out of range, and let's get the other cargo ship to Shanghai safely." Leslie and his crew put their stretcher up and secured it. As he was going back to the dayroom, he ran into the XO. "Sir, may I ask a question?"

"Sure," said the XO, "ask away, Sailor."

"Sir, I know why I'm not issued a rifle. I can't carry it and a stretcher at the same time, but I could wear a sidearm. It would not get in the way."

"Sailor, the reason we don't issue stretcher bearers a side arm, we want them only to think about their job of helping the wounded. We do not want you to ever think about getting into a gunfight. We also don't arm medical people or the ship's firemen. They have a job to do. Do you understand what I'm talking about?"

"Yes, sir."

"As you were, Sailor."

"Aye, aye, sir," replies Leslie. The *Guam* did a fast turnaround and resupplied in Shanghai to escort the second cargo ship with its marines up the river to Hung Ho, where they had off boarded the first marines and their equipment. Leslie kept himself busy in the machine shop and doing repairs around the ship. Just before the *Guam* rounded the bend at Hung Ho, the captain had the men armed again and told the crew to be on alert, to be ready for anything. Off boarding the marines and guarding the cargo ship when it docked went off with a hitch. The men could hear gunshots off in the distance up the river but not close.

The XO told them, "The tankers and their escort are getting close. Whoever is shooting at them would like to stop and board them before they get to us, so be ready." The *Guam* headed out to the middle of the river as soon as it saw the tankers coming down toward them. As the tankers passed the *Guam*, the *Guam* went to help the USS *Tutuila*. The pirates were firing on the *Tutuila*. She was getting shot up pretty bad. The *Guam* fired a three-inch shell at the first junk chasing the *Tutuila*. It struck the bow of the junk and blew off the whole front of the junk. The rest of the flotilla chasing the *Tutuila* turned and headed away from the Tutuila and the tankers. The captain of the *Guam* thanked his men for a well-executed maneuver. They were able to break up the attack on the convoy and not take any hits themselves. The *Guam* then steamed to the front of the convoy to lead it to Shanghai. Three trips up the river and three trips back in three weeks with all of the loading and unloading and the attacks and no one was hurt. This cruise was considered a great success. Leslie and McGhee were assigned to the shipyard to work the repairs on the *Tutuila*. In a week the *Tutuila* was ordered to steam back up the Yangtze to where it usually patrolled. The area commander let the men of the *Tutuila* stay in Shanghai that week and have liberty daily. He felt that the men deserved a rest. Leslie and McGhee were to stay with the *Tutuila* and keep working repairs until they got to Zigui, where their house and their girls were. The trip took three days. In Zigui the boys walked to the path where there house was, and the girls were outside tending to a garden. As soon as the girls saw them, they ran to them. They all kissed and hugged each other. Lechou and the Russian kept talking and kissing the boys. Leslie noticed that his Russian was speaking some Chinese. Leslie still could not understand her since he did not speak Chinese. He was glad she was beginning to communicate with Lechou. Now maybe he could know her name. When everybody settled down, the group went into the house. It looked great. The girls had spent the last two months painting and decorating. It was beginning to look like a very nice and cozy home.

Hojoh knocked on the door and came in. "Good to see you, bosses," he cried. And they all shook hands. "How long you be home for?" Hojoh asked.

"Four days," replied Leslie. He really liked the sound of saying "home." Leslie took his Russian into her room and sat her on the bed. He gave her a wrapped gift. She took the gift and slowly opened it.

CHAPTER 13

RAIN

I t was a very nice music box. It had a ballerina that turned on it, and it softly played, "Beautiful Dreamer." The Russian started crying when she heard it. Leslie hugged her and kissed her on the top of the head. Leslie took her hand in his and tapped himself on the chest and said, "Leslie." He then touched her chest. She did not say anything, so he tapped his chest again, saying, "Leslie." He again touched her chest.

She shook her head up and down and said, "Rain."

Leslie repeated it. "Rain."

She said yes and nodded her head up and down. Rain, what a nice name. It means, fresh, clean, nice, and warm, that is if he is pronouncing it the right way. It sounded like "rain" anyway.

Hojoh asked, "Boss, you want to go somewhere?"

"No," answered Leslie, "I want to stay home tonight. We'll tour around tomorrow."

Lechou told Rain something in Chinese, and the girls left for the market. McGhee looked in the footlocker that he had left at the house when they went back the first time to see if any of the beers he had put in there were still there, and yes, they were.

He opened a beer for him and Leslie and said, "Cheers." He then cut eight strings, three feet long, and tied one end of each to the necks of the beer bottles. He then tied the other end to a long piece of bamboo and stuck the beers in the little creek that ran behind the garden. The beers would be cool in a short while. The boys found some of the dried fish to munch on while drinking there beers. *This was the good life.*

Lechou and Rain came back from the market and started to prepare the evening meal. The boys sat out on the bench in front of their home and talked to Hojoh and his brother about the war. It was evident that the brothers were not on the same side. Hojoh seem to side with the Communists, and his brother seemed to side with Chiang Kai-shek's nationalists. Both the brothers hated the Japanese. Houle, Hojoh's brother kept talking about Americans sending arms to the Communists and that the nationalists had to buy their weapons from the British. The Japanese had taken most of the eastern seaboard of China and were beginning to take a few cities. The war had started in Manchuria and the Japanese just kept on coming. Chiang could not stop the Communists and the Japanese at the same time. He had already lost a large part of his officer core, especially the young, well-trained, and politically correct officers. The American government was supplying the nationalists and the Communists. We also had sanctions against the Japanese and were beginning to have problems with the Russians supplying the Communists. The Communists were being trained politically by the Russians, and their officers were training the Communist officers and men. It was a mess, politically and militarily. Chiang had spent a decade conquering and subduing the warlords of China to bring the country under one rule. He was establishing a single language of the dozen spoken and trying to increase exports and centralizing education. Spending all the time trying to "country build" had cost him men and money. He was trying to eradicate the Communists. Chiang had spent months in Moscow studying their ways and decided in was not right for China.

The girls came back from the market carrying flowers and fresh food to prepare. Lechou and Rain went to the garden to their outside stove and started to work. They washed and sang and chopped and danced. They were having a good time with the men being home. Leslie could smell the food, and it smelled great. From the smell he knew Lechou was fixing grilled bok choy and paddlefish, his favorite. Rain brought out a bowl of sliced mangoes and star fruit and lychee; it was cool and sweet. Rain came out and motioned for them to come to the garden to eat. The food was delicious. The fish was grilled with a hot spice. It was hot and moist and very good. The grilled bok choy was perfect. They had rice with a thick chicken-tasting black-pepper gravy. The beer was cold and there was plenty of it. When the meal was finished and they cleaned up the garden, Rain took Leslie by the hand and took him to her room. The tub was full of hot water and the lamps down low. As Leslie undressed, he realized this was the second time he had been naked in front of her alone. He also realized that she was the only woman he had ever been naked in front of. He wasn't sure if he was embarrassed or if he liked her looking at him naked. When his bath was finished, it was time for hers. What passion, oh, what a night. Rain kept playing the music box all night.

The boys woke up late, 9:00 a.m. The girls had breakfast ready for them—eggs, sardines, fruit, and hot coffee. Leslie thought to himself, *I could live like this the rest of my life.* He felt warm, full, and relaxed. McGhee wanted to go fishing. They had tried before but got shot at, which ended their fishing trip. Leslie agreed. They would try fishing again.

"Hojoh, tell your cousin to get the sampan. We would like to try fishing again, on this side of the river, okay?"

"Sure, boss, I tell him. He just live right here." He pointed to a hut just across the path. Lechou and Rain packed a picnic for the four of them. She packed, sardines, fruit, and beer. They loaded up the sampan and pulled their way up a small stream, about twenty feet across and three or four feet deep. Hojoh got the boys some bamboo poles and fishing lines and hooks. They baited their hooks with sardines and started fishing. Leslie was the first one to catch something. It was a turtle. He unhooked it and let it go.

Lechou said, "No no." She pointed to the turtle swimming away and then to her mouth and then to her stomach and rubbed her stomach and said, "Good."

Leslie understood. He and McGhee caught lots of small fish but nothing they wanted. When finally Leslie caught a big turtle again, he said, "I'll swear, I think this is the same old turtle I caught this morning."

"Looks the same to me," added McGhee. They had a good laugh. McGhee caught another large turtle and they kept it too. They caught an eight pounder that look like a catfish but uglier. They kept it too. Lechou pointed out birds that they saw and told them their Chinese names. The birds were beautiful; most of them Leslie had never seen before. Lechou would again point to her mouth and then stomach on about half the birds. Leslie realized that the Chinese would eat about anything. He realized he also never saw any farm animals except pigs or chickens. He had heard of ducks but had never seen one. Had they eaten everything else? Probably so. Leslie kept watching a very tall crane. He probably stood six feet and weighted in at about twenty pounds. He had a bright red head, a white body and black tail feathers, very long orange legs, and he was catching fish bigger than the ones they were catching. He could swallow them right down. He wondered what he was called. Leslie asked Lechou by pointing to it. She motioned to her mouth and shook her head no. Leslie pointed to the bird and said the name. He pointed to himself and said, "Leslie." Then he pointed to her and said, "Lechou." And then he then pointed to the bird again. Lechou nodded her head yes, that she understood, and said something in Chinese. Leslie still could not understand her. *Oh well, I'll just call it the tall crane*, he thought to himself. It really was a majestic-looking bird. The group pulled on upstream and came to some rice fields and a farmer plowing. He was using a water buffalo to pull the plow.

McGhee said, "What a picture. You know we should buy a camera and take some pictures."

Leslie responded and said, "Man, you're right. Look at all that we have seen and done, and we have nothing to show people or to look at to bring back some great memories when we get back to the port. I'll start looking for cameras. I got another one." Leslie pulled a large turtle into the boat.

"We have enough fish and turtles. Let's drift back to Yangtze and go home," said McGhee.

"Let's do it," said Leslie, and downstream they drifted. As they drifted, Leslie kept pointing to the tall cranes for Rain to see. The trip back took about two hours, and by the time they got back the beer was gone and they were all hungry.

Lechou took the fish and wrapped them in wet paper, put the paper in a big bowl, put the bowl in the very cold running creek, put a plate on top of the bowl as a lid, and put a rock on the plate. Leslie understood that this would keep the fish fresh a couple of days, the same way they cooled down the beers, using the cold water in the creek. Lechou took the turtle and Rain to the back garden and started to prepare them for the evening meal. The boys washed and cleaned themselves up and put on fresh, ironed, clean clothes and sat on the front bench and told Hojoh of their adventure. Leslie had on Chinese sandals, he got to where he liked them very much. He had never worn sandals in America. He actually did not know any man who did. Rain called them to the garden to eat. They had turtle soup with green onions and noodles. They had turtle meat on long bamboo skewers grilled. They had fried vegetables in a thick, clear gravy. And for fruit, they had skewered grilled pears and star fruit. Leslie had never eaten turtle before and decided that it may be his favorite meat. It tasted as good as his mother's cook Ruth's pork chops. All around the table and garden were papers folded to look like cranes. You could pull their feet and the head would move.

Wow, where did they get these? thought Leslie. He looked at the cranes and decided he could not ever make them. Lechou took a piece of paper and folded it into a crane. "Wow," said Leslie. He looked at Lechou and asked, "What is this called?"

Lechou nodded her head, saying she understood. "Origami," she said. She then took another piece of paper and made a different bird. Lechou gave the boys and Rain a piece of paper and showed them how to make a flower, and then they made a boat, another bird, and another flower.

This was a good day—fishing, sightseeing, eating, drinking beer, and doing origami.

The next morning there were two Japanese gunboats steaming up the river slowly. They were loaded with soldiers. The people of the village kept very quiet and stayed in their homes.

Hojoh came into Leslie's home and said, "Boss, Japanese here. Stay inside."

"What do they want?" Leslie asked. "Don't know, boss. Whatever it is, it not good." The Japanese steamed on up the river. The people of Zigui started coming out of their homes and other buildings. They all headed to the markets by the river. Everyone was talking at once. Hojoh tried to translate for Leslie and McGhee, but the people were talking so fast, and there were so many of them. Hojoh just looked at Leslie. He did not have to say anything. Leslie knew that the people of the village were scared. The Japanese controlled parts of the land north of the river, as far inland to the Huangshi province. The Japanese could navigate the river without much fear of the Chinese navy. There wasn't much of one, and it could not compete with the Japanese navy, which was one of the most powerful. The people of the town started getting prepared for the Japanese to march into Zigui. Leslie and McGhee started helping Lechou and Rain gather foods and supplies. Leslie dug three holes. He rolled their paper money into small tight rolls and put them into bottles. He sealed the bottles with corks and put each one in a hole by itself. He buried the holes and put flat walking rocks on top of them. They blended in with the walkway in the garden. They purchased lots of dried fish and dried vegetables. Leslie buried about forty bottles of beer on the creek bed. It could not be seen. McGhee hid a couple of gallons of fuel oil for the lamps in the marsh behind the house. Everything was ready for the Japanese invasion. That night Lechou retrieved the fish in the bowl in the creek. She and Rain grilled the flesh of the fish and boiled the rest—heads, tails, fins, innards—and made a soup with noodles and chopped vegetables. Lechou grilled some bok choy, one of Leslie's favorites.

That night was a night of passion for Leslie and Rain. They seemed to know that their time together was not going to last long. For breakfast they had the rest of the fish and some fruit. While eating they heard the villagers explode in talk and hollering and running and shouting. Leslie told the girls to stay in the house, and he, Houle, Hojoh's brother, Hojoh, and McGhee ran down to the docks. The Japanese gunboats were back and one of them was at the dock. Japanese soldiers were walking through the market picking up great quantities of food and was taking it to their ship without offering to pay for it. They were grabbing livestock, fresh fish on tables, and beer and wine. They grabbed full baskets of fruit and vegetables, and if a merchant tried to stop them, he was thrown to the ground and stomped. They also grabbed young girls and put them on the gunboats. Everybody was screaming and running, but the Japanese just kept looting. This gunboat steamed back to the middle of the river, where it shared its loot with the other gunboat. And then they steamed back downriver. Leslie was glad his house was many hundreds yards up from the river. This would keep them safe from these kinds of raids, and he was sure there would be more. The Sino-Japanese was now about eighteen months old, and the carnage was devastating. By now Chiang has lost three hundred thousand soldiers, and the Communists had lost about two hundred thousand. Civilian deaths were also about three hundred thousand women and children.

The boys got up early on the fifth day and packed to head back to Shanghai. Leslie hugged Rain and she cried. He actually had a little mist in his eyes. He knew he had to see her again. He loved her.

The trip back down the river was an eye-opener. Leslie had really never seen war. On the way back to Shanghai, they observed two of the little villages about the size of Zigui were burned to the ground, the docks were burned, and so were a lot of the sampans. As far as they could see, all the people had left. There were bodies on the banks of the river and what was left of any docks, then there was the smell of rotten, animals, vegetables, people—oh what a sight. The smell caused many of the sailors to be sick. More got sick when they saw what happens to a human body as it rots in water. This was a terrible sight. The captain ordered the ship to go "full speed ahead." The ship hit bodies of dead Chinese and of animals. A very large water buffalo was swollen up and ready to explode from decaying, and the human bodies had very large stomachs from decomposing. It took the gunboat an hour to get away from all the carnage. Leslie swore he would never get over the smell. The captain ordered the fire hose turned on the boat, and he wanted the boat scrubbed down. He wanted it GI'd (ready for a general inspection). The crew worked on cleaning the ship all day. Everything was washed and polished and shined. The captain had the ship aired out. He did not want to smell any bad odors. He allowed, for the first time, the men to light Chinese incense. He, the captain, wanted any lingering odors of the river gone.

The captain was a third-generation navy man. His dad was the XO of an old Great War battlewagon. He had died just as his son graduated from the University of Chicago. His granddad had been a warrant officer in the Spanish-American War. The captain, whose name is Emory C. Tanner, loved the navy and everything it stood for. He was thirty years old and hoped to command one of the larger fighting ships. He was pretty sure we would be fighting the Japanese soon, and he wanted to be out in the Pacific in a great naval battle, commanding the lead battleship. Captain Tanner knew he could make a difference in his command. He would receive lot of glory and promotions. He figured he could make admiral in ten to twelve more years. His men respected and trusted him. He ran a tight ship the navy way, and his men were well trained and professional. He did not like the beards on the men but knew he was not going to be able to change that policy since half of his officers and warrant officers have facial hair of some kind. The captain had all of his clothes tailored, and he always looked like a poster child for naval officers; the man was sharp. Leslie told McGhee that the captain reminded him of his favorite uncle, Franz—same big smile, big bright white teeth, and a look in his eyes that told you that he is one to watch. You don't want to cross him.

The cruise was finally over, and the boys were at their home port. It had been a hard cruise, one they would not forget. Leslie had been in China a little over a year, and he wanted to go home, at least for a visit. He asked the XO if he could have leave to go home for a couple of weeks.

The XO told him, "Seaman, to go home to North Carolina from China and stay a couple of weeks, it will take about three weeks to get home and three weeks to get back at the best, and to stay home anytime, it will take about two and a half, maybe three months. Do you have that kind of time saved up?"

"No, sir."

"Well, Seaman, here's what you have to figure out—somehow a cruise to the West Coast then some kind of ride to the mountains of western North Carolina, and then all that in reverse to get back."

"Well, sir, if I can get to the West Coast, I can hope a train to Asheville free and then another train back to the West Coast."

"What makes you think you could just hop a train? Are you an ex-hobo, Seaman?"

"Sir, my dad works for the railroad and he'll arrange it."

"Oh," said the XO. "Now we have to work on the trip from here to the West Coast and back. Do you have any ideas on that?"

"Well, yes, sir. I'll need to find a ship going to the West Coast, who will be docked about two weeks and is going to return to China, then I could hop a ship back to here. I'll need to find a ship that needs a welder for the trip or just a deck hand."

"Well, Seaman, that sound like a good plan, but it's going to be hard to find a ship like that," replied the XO. "I'll ask around for you. Just be patient, okay?"

"Yes, sir."

Leslie went back to his job in the machine shop. He really did not have anything to do right now, so to keep from being bored and to look like he was working, he decided to make a steel crane, like the one's he saw in the marshes. Leslie wanted this crane to be life-size. He sat and drew it out and figured he could make it in about two days. McGhee came in to the shop and asked what he was making, Leslie told him, "A crane, like we have at home," meaning the little hut in Zigui. McGhee said, "What a great idea. I think I'll make a cup rack and a plate rack and maybe a hanging pot rack to go in the house also." The boys started working on their home projects and had a great time. Sailors on ships were always bored and always found different projects to occupy their time. There was painting, writing, carving, playing music, playing cards, and reading. Leslie did his steel sculptures and played music. Time went by fast for him. Eight weeks had passed before the *Guam* steamed up the Yangtze River as far as Zigui. Leslie and McGhee finally got to go back upriver to their little home and their ladies.

Zigui was on hard times. The wars, the Japanese, and bandits continued to fight around the province. Most commerce had had to stop. The poor farmers were being killed every time they tried to work in their fields. Nobody really shot at them, but stray bullets and bombs seemed to take its toll on them. Most of the foreign military were told not to get involved, to stay alert, and do their jobs. The *Guam* escorted Chinese junks full of American weapons and supplies to Chiang's forces around that part of the river. The American government did not have much faith in Chiang's army stopping the Japanese or the Communists, but maybe he could cause a stalemate and get some of the fighting to stop.

The mail finally caught up to the *Guam*, and Leslie received his much-needed mail from Asheville. He read is mom's letter first. She first told him of his brothers and sisters, how they were doing, and then about her and his father. She told him of a dinner party they had with the Scrounces—Katie and her brother and her mother—and that Franz had come and had Suzie Davis with him. Brigitta told him how much she liked the two girls, Katie and Suzie, and how much fun the party was. Franz was still Franz, and she did not know what Suzie saw in him. Brigitta hated to say it, but she was sure Franz was a gangster and so was his friend Mr. Daddy Rabbit. She told Leslie that she was sure Suzie Davis did not know this, that Suzie had come from a respectable family and they would not associate with a gangster. Brigitta told Leslie that she had heard the rumor of Franz throwing Suzie's first husband off of a bridge and killing him over a gambling debt. Brigitta also sent Leslie some newer pictures of the kids and of her and Otto. Leslie then opened his letter from Katie. Katie told him of her love and that he needed to get home soon. Her heart was breaking to see him. This letter made him a little sad. He knew he loved her, but he knew he also loved Rain. He also thought back to his mother's letter. He had never thought of Franz as a gangster, but come to think of it, he probably was, and so was Daddy Rabbit. Leslie thought, *I would love to see both of them again.*

McGhee came by the shop and asked Leslie if he was ready to go see the girls.

Leslie thought to himself, *No, I don't need to cheat on Katie anymore, and I'm not going to.* He replied, "Sure, let's go." They grabbed their weekend bags, and off they went to their little piece of heaven. Leslie took three steel cranes, two other steel birds, three steel flowers, and a steel wind arrow. McGhee had all his steel home decor with him. After a good walk home, the stuff got very heavy. Leslie noticed a lot of automobile traffic and foot traffic in the city. He noticed a lot of makeshift shelters on every street. He figured refugees from the country were streaming into the city from their farms, looking for safety. There were hundreds of nationalist soldiers wandering around the town also. Leslie began to feel uneasy about being on the streets. Finally he and McGhee got to their little home safely. The girls were very glad to see them. Leslie took Rain out to the garden and the marsh and planted his art works, the steel birds and flowers. McGhee installed his household pot and china holders. They looked great. Lechou came into the garden and looked at Leslie's art and hugged him. The girls changed into clean clothes, and the group went to the market to buy some food. Leslie noticed that the market was full of people trying to sell everything—clothes, weapons, household supplies, art work, and tools. Leslie also noticed there was not as much food at the market as usual. Leslie ran into Hojoh at the market, pulling a Chinese officer in his rickshaw. When they saw each other, Hojoh looked at Leslie and slightly shook his head no. Leslie understood he was not to talk to Hojoh or even act like he knew him. Leslie knew that the nationalist Chinese did not care for or trust the Americans, even with the Americans supplying Chiang's army.

The girls squealed, so Leslie went over to them. They were pointing to little furry animals. The animals were about ten inches long and had little tails.

Lechou said, "Buy, buy." Leslie nodded his head yes. Lechou started talking to the lady who ran this table at the market. Lechou turned to Leslie and stuck out her hand for money. Leslie gave her a bag of Chinese coins. He had been collecting Chinese coins for the last month. He had two bags full, each one about the size of his fist. Lechou took the bag and handed the lady a couple of the coins. To Leslie's horror, the lady took a hammer and smacked each of the four little furry animals in the head and killed them. He thought the girls were buying the little animals as pets. Now he figured out they were for food.

McGhee said, "Will you eat them?"

Leslie said, "Sure, I've eaten plenty of squirrels and rabbits. I think they're about the same kind of thing, don't you?"

"I suppose so," said McGhee. The group kept shopping and bought some vegetables for about double the price they were a couple of months ago. Leslie also bought a burlap bag of apples. The guys noticed that most people would not make eye contact with them. Everybody seemed a little standoffish to them now. McGhee purchased a large burlap bag of rice beer, and it was also high priced. The group went back to the house, and the ladies prepared the meal. They had grilled meat. Lechou had gutted the animals and skinned them. She flattened them out and put them on the grill. She had little squares of some kind of dough and put the hearts, four of them on four pieces of dough. She then pinched the dough close and dropped them in hot oil to cook. She did the same for their livers. They also had chopped and fried vegetables in a sauce. The beer was cool and the meat was great.

Hojoh came into the house. He wanted to explain to Leslie about the Chinese officer. "Boss Leslie, the nationalist officer don't like foreigners. He would rob me if he thought I like American sailors."

"That's okay, Hojoh, we understand the politics of it. Would you like some dinner?" asked Leslie.

"Sure, Boss, I love (whatever he called the meat in Chinese)."

"Hojoh, what is this called in American?" asked Leslie.

"Bamboo rat," replied Hojoh.

"Rat? Did he say *rat?*" asked McGhee.

"I don't think it's like the kind of rats we're used to. I think these are more like squirrels," replied Leslie. "Whatever they were, they tasted good." The night was cool and smelled good. The boys got bathed and rubbed down, and then they gave their girls their bath. Leslie had a very good night. He woke up to the smell of eggs cooking and of fish grilling. They had a very good breakfast. Without Hojoh to show them around and to translate, they did not know what to do.

Leslie took Rain and Lechou to the garden and buried the other sack, or sock, of coins. The girls took the guys to a chicken fight. Leslie had been to a chicken fight or cockfight once before. Leslie wondered why the girls wanted to see chickens kill each other. It was a sight—people betting and getting into fight themselves, cocks fighting and feathers everywhere. The handlers of the chicken would tie little knives, called gaffs, to the chicken legs. This inflicted cuts and blinded some of the combatants.

Lechou was where the dead birds were piled up, talking to the handlers. She came over to Leslie and held her hand out for money, saying, "Buy." Leslie gave her the bag of coins, and she purchased two dead roosters. Now Leslie understood they were having chicken tonight for dinner. As they walked around the market, Rain pulled the feathers from the dead birds and let them fall to the ground.

By the time they got home, Rain had plucked out all the feathers from one chicken and was halfway done with the other one. Lechou took all the innards out of the birds and cooked them, and then she grilled the cocks with their heads and feet still attached to body's. They looked a little gross but tasted just fine. Rain wanted Leslie to try the chicken feet again, but he declined. McGhee gnawed on one of the feet. He seemed to really like it. Leslie thought about the Southern fried chicken Ruth, his mother's cook, would fix, with dumpling and gravy and homemade biscuits. He could close his eyes and taste it. He turned in for the night, and Rain came with him. He held her most of the night.

Leslie and McGhee had to catch a British gunboat headed to Shanghai to get back to work on time. They would meet the *Guam* in about a day and a half on their way downriver and the *Guam* would be on its way up. They boys could hear fighting and big guns firing but did not see any. A lot of the small villages along the river had been burned to the ground. The river was full of sampans and junks full of people headed to Shanghai.

Japanese planes were flying over them all day. You could look up and see the bombs hooked to the planes going upriver. The plane coming back down would be bombless. The war was getting closer to them every day.

When Leslie got back on the *Guam*, the XO came to see him. "Seaman, I may have been able to find you a way home. A battleship is going to San Francisco by way of Pearl Harbor. The trip will take about two weeks. She will be in port about two weeks and then return on the same route. Are you interested?"

"Hell yes—sorry, sir. I mean yes, sir," answered Leslie. "When is it going to happen, sir?"

"About a week. I thought you would jump at it, so we are already cutting you orders. Is that okay, Seaman?"

"Yes, sir."

"Now this is not a vacation for you. They need a couple of welders and machinist mates for some work on their ship," said the XO.

"That's fine, sir. I'm not afraid of work," replied Leslie. As soon as they got to the port of Shanghai, Leslie wired his dad of his trip home. His new ship was to leave China in four days. This gave him time to buy gifts for the family and for Katie and her mother. He got his laundry done and he got a haircut and a shave. Leslie's new orders came in, and he was to report to the new ship two days before it left port.

CHAPTER 14

THE CRUISE HOME

L eslie reported to the ship. He could not believe how big it was. It had a crew of over seven hundred men. Leslie met his new shipmates and was shown his duty assignments. There was enough welding for months. At least the time would pass quickly with all that had to be done. This ship had plenty of sailors who had musical instruments. He was able to play with different people and different types of music. The cruise to Pearl Harbor was smooth and uneventful. Leslie worked hard and played a lot of music.

There was a wire waiting for him when the ship docked. It said "aloha" and gave him a phone number to call. What was this about? Leslie did not know anyone in Hawaii. He found a pay phone and called the number.

"Gift shop" was the answer on the phone.

"Hello," said Leslie, "I was told to call this number."

"Leslie Charles, Brigitta's son?" was the answer he got.

"Yes," he said, "who is this?"

"My goodness, it's nice to hear your voice. I'm Woodley Patton, I'm your second cousin. I'm Brigitta's first cousin. Your mom wired us that you were coming to Pearl Harbor and told us to look out for you."

"You're my mom's cousin and you live in Hawaii," replied Leslie. "I'm sorry, but I do not know you, and you live here?"

"Yes, we do now. I was in the army stationed at Hickam Field. When I got out we moved here to settle down, been here about a year," said Woodley Patton. "Now, Leslie, I want you to get a taxi and come to the Royal Hawaiian Hotel gift shop in Honolulu. I'll be waiting for you, okay?"

"Okay." Leslie caught a taxi and off he went to a new adventure. When he arrived at the hotel, he asked for the gift shop. A bellman pointed to it and Leslie headed that way. A couple came out of the gift shop and stuck out their hands to shake his. "Leslie?" they asked. "We're Alma and Woodley Patton, your cousins."

"Hello, it's nice to meet you," replied Leslie, and they all shook hands.

"Come on into the store and we'll get you settled in," said Alma. Leslie followed them in. "Now, son, tell us all about yourself and your family."

Leslie took almost an hour telling them about his family and about himself. Alma served him pineapple juice and then coconut milk. He had pineapple cookies and some kind of nut called macadamia nuts. Boy, it was all good.

Leslie asked, "Now how did you all get here in Hawaii?"

"Well, let me see," said Woodley. "I was born and raised outside of Sweetwater, Tennessee. I was about twenty-one. Way before most of the Depression hit Tennessee, there were no jobs and no future for me, so I joined the army. My first duty was in Panama, three years. Wow, was it hot! My next duty was in Fort Hood, Texas, two years. I met Alma and her husband, Chet, at my next assignment at Fort Bragg, two years in North Carolina. Both Chet and I were assigned to the army air corps field here in Hawaii. We were both in the motor pool. We stayed here for four years and we became great friends. Alma spent four years trying to fix me up with her lady friends. Alma and Chet went back to Fort Bragg and I went Fort Myers in Virginia. I finally made E5 after I was there a year. Chet was still E4, and he had about the same time in as I did. Chet died of a heatstroke in North Carolina. I got leave to drive down to be in his funeral. Alma and I stayed friends and wrote to each other for the next year. Chet and Alma were from Wilmington, North Carolina, and she moved home. I got reassigned to Fort Bragg and Alma and I started seeing each other. I got to Hawaii again and I asked Alma to come out here with me and we got married and she moved here. After four years the army wanted me to go back to Panama. Alma and I talked about it and decided we would stay in Hawaii. I had saved a lot of money, and with Chet's insurance money, Alma and I bought this store and a little hut just off the grounds of the hotel, and we've been here and happy for a while. This is a great life."

"How long are you going to be able to stay with us?" Alma asked Leslie.

"I can stay two nights, and then it's back to the ship and to the States," answered Leslie. That evening when they closed the store at 1900 hours, they walked Leslie to their home. The outside looked like a large grass hut. The insides were different. It had a modern kitchen and bath. It had two bedrooms and a very large living area that open to a large screened-in deck with views of the ocean. What a nice home. Most of the furniture was made from bamboo; it really looked neat. Leslie got up the next morning to a great breakfast of fresh fruit and juice and bacon and eggs with real buttered toast. Alma went to work at the gift shop, and Woodley took Leslie to the beach and then to a pineapple farm. Leslie got to pick a ripe pineapple for their lunch with a real pork chop and green beans and potatoes and gravy. Woodley took Leslie to a real Hawaiian village with real Hawaiians (the real natives). They drove up on one of the mountains or volcanoes and looked down on Pearl Harbor. Leslie was really impressed with the size of the harbor and all the big ships in it. There were so many big ships with big guns that Leslie thought to himself, *Nobody will ever mess with them.* That evening Alma gave Leslie a Hawaiian shirt to put on. It was silk and had bright flowers on it. The Pattons took Leslie to a large luau. (A luau is a lawn party, with Hawaiian food and entertainment.) They had cooked a berried pig, had a paste called poi, little grilled fish, grilled fruit, and grilled vegetables. Girls came out in grass skirts and danced. The men had on crowns from palm leaves and played the drums. Everything was lit by torches. Some of the men blew through big seashells and made horn noises. It was quite a party. Leslie had the best time.

The last morning in Hawaii he went early to the gift shop with Alma and Woodley. He bought four grass skirts, two for his sisters and one each for his mom and one for Katie. He got his dad a Hawaiian shirt and his brothers chess men made from lava rock. He also got Franz and Daddy Rabbit switchblade knives made with bamboo handles. The shop had everything from Hawaii—shell horns made from conch shells, painted shells, salt-and-pepper shakers made from every product in Hawaii or painted with Hawaiian scenes, every kind of pineapple jelly or jam or syrup, grass skirts and flower leis, jewelry, pictures, books, all kinds of products made from bamboo, products made from lava rock, towels with the hotel name on them, and playing cards with all kinds of Hawaiian scenes on them. This was a great store. Leslie said his good-byes and boarded his ship.

The cruise to San Francisco was also quiet and the time passed quickly. When Leslie signed off the ship, he headed to the railroad station. Once there, he went to the telegraph and teletype office. He told the men who he was. They had been expecting him. In an hour he was on a cargo train headed east. He rode in the caboose for the first day. The train got to Denver the first day. Leslie boarded a passenger train the second day. He got to ride in comfort and have some decent chow. He got into Memphis on the second day and was back on an empty coal train to Asheville on the third day.

Leslie stepped off the train and there were his parents. He was so happy to see them. It had been a little over a year. They all hugged and headed home. He got home and was unpacked by the time the kids got home. Albert was in from Mars Hill College, and John Henry was attending the new Asheville-Biltmore College. Franz came walking in with Suzie Davis on his arm.

Brigitta whispered to Leslie, "I did not know he was even out of bed. It's 3:00 p.m., and he's usually asleep at this time of day."

Leslie laughed.

He and Franz hugged and he then hugged Suzie. Franz asked, "Do you need my car to pick up Katie?" He threw Leslie the keys.

"Thanks, Franz. I'm going to get her now. You guys can come if you want to," replied Leslie.

"Sure," said Suzie, "let's go."

"Mom, come on and go with us," said Leslie.

"No, you go and bring her back here. We're going to get dinner on," said his mom.

Leslie and Franz and Suzie Davis got in the car and headed to pick up Katie at Lee Edward High School. Katie and Leslie met each other at the front steps under the rotunda. They hugged and kissed. The student who saw them whistled. In the car on the way to his parents' home they kissed and hugged a lot.

At his folks' home, Leslie started passing out his gifts. His mom and Katie put their grass skirts on over their dresses. His dad put on his Hawaiian shirt. Leslie gave his brothers and sisters their gifts. He gave Suzie Davis a tortoise shell comb, he gave Franz his switchblade, and he gave Ruth and her sister salt-and-pepper shakers. And last, he also gave Katie a string of pearls, which made Katie cry. Everybody grabbed their musical instruments and they all started to play. As they played, Little Herbert stuck his hand in his armpit and pumped his arm to make sounds. He could keep time doing that, but his mother grabbed his arm and told him to quit. Everybody laughed. Otto said, "You know, we now call him Herbert the Horrible." Everybody laughed again.

Ruth came out and said, "Dinner is ready. I made something special for Mr. Leslie." She served kill salad (leaf lettuce with sliced spring onions and white vinegar) at the dinner table. Just before serving, she poured very hot bacon grease with bits of bacon in it on the salad. It popped and fried right in the bowl. You want to eat it hot. Man, was it good. Next she served spaghetti with red sauce and breaded veal cutlets. She served brussels sprout with apple cider vinegar. They had garlic toast with grated Romano cheese. For dessert Ruth served spumoni. Everyone ate until they were stuffed.

During the meal, Leslie told stories of China and the men he worked with and all the different fish, birds, and animals he had seen and tasted. He did not tell them of the two times he was robbed or of Rain. He was going to tell all that to Franz when they were alone. He did tell them that he did not see any dogs or cats in China and that he suspected that the Chinese had eaten them all. He talked to his mom about her cousins in Hawaii and how nice they were to him. At 10:00 p.m., Katie told him she had to go home, that she had to teach tomorrow. Franz and Suzie said they would ride along to take Katie home. When they got to the middle of town, Franz told Leslie to take him and Suzie to Daddy Rabbit's first, and then he could take Katie home. Leslie pulled into Daddy's place and Franz said, "We'll be here when you get back. Take your time. Good to see you, Katie." Leslie drove Katie to the bottom of Hilendale Street. Katie slid over to him and said, "How many kisses will you give me?" And she gave him a lot. He walked her to her door, and they said there I love yous, and he got into the car and left. He drove the back to Daddy Rabbit's. He was so worked up he had to stop the car and relieve himself of all the pressure in his loins.

He arrived at Daddy Rabbit's and he was tired. He went into Daddy Rabbit's, and everyone in the place treated him like a conquering hero. There were handshakes and pats on the back. Daddy Rabbit came out and gave Leslie a big hug. Leslie was almost in tears with the welcome they gave him. Leslie gave Daddy the switchblade he got for him in Hawaii. Franz and Suzie came over from the dance floor, and they all sat at a table where Leslie told China stories. He told some of the war stories he did not tell at the dinner table.

Leslie said to Franz, "It's late and I'm really tired. Can you take me home?"

"Can you ride a motorcycle?"

"I've not ridden one since you taught me," he replied.

"Here, take the Indian," said Franz and threw Leslie the keys.

"You're going to let me ride the Indian?" asked Leslie.

"Only you, Leslie. He won't even me ride it," stated Daddy Rabbit.

Leslie got on the Indian and started for home. *Damn, it's cold,* he thought to himself. When he got home, he thought he was going to have to be helped into the house. He was frozen stiff.

Leslie got up early to take the kids to school and his mother on her rounds. He took his mom out to the soda shop on Pack Square for lunch. They both had hamburgers with french fries on them and strawberry milkshakes. He took his mother home and went to the rail yard to play music with his dad. While he was there, he had to tell his war stories to the railroad men. He had to describe the food and the fishing trips he had taken—both trips, the one where they were shot at and the one where he caught turtles to eat. Some of the men asked him if he thought we would go to war with the Japanese. Leslie said he thought that it may happen.

Some of the railroad men said the same thing that other people had said. The Japanese were too small and could not see very well and that they all had bucked teeth.

Leslie told them, "The Japanese soldiers I saw were well trained, well armed and supplied. They did not need glasses and were the size of an average man. They have already taken Korea and now half of China. They have a bigger navy than we do and a very large air corps. These men know how to fight."

"What can we do?" asked some of the men.

"Right now we're—that's is, the American government—is supplying the Chinese nationalist army, and I think we're still helping the Chinese Communists. If they can put up a good enough fight, the Japanese won't have time to fight us," added Leslie. Leslie told them of the village on the river that they passed that had been destroyed and about all the thousands of bodies, humans and animals, rotting in the river.

Leslie told his dad he had to leave, that he had to pick up the kids from school. He picked up all the kids and took them home, and then he went and picked up Katie at school. He took Katie home, and her mother was just getting home when they pulled up.

Leslie took his gift in for Mrs. Scrounce, salt-and-pepper shakers and a tortoise shell comb. She loved them and told Leslie so. She made iced tea and cookies for them. He got to tell her the stories of China and Hawaii, the good stories and not anything upsetting. Mrs. Scrounce made them BLTs and grilled cheese and fried potatoes for dinner. She also had some homemade bread and butter pickles. He and Katie sat on the porch swing and talked of future plans. They kissed and hugged each other. At 10:00 p.m., Mrs. Scrounce came out of the house to wish Leslie a good night, which meant it was time for him to leave. He and Katie said good night and Leslie went to Daddy Rabbit's.

There he ran into Franz and Daddy. They had a beer and talked. He now told them of Rain and asked what to do. He felt so guilty.

"No no, don't feel guilty about it. This is good for you and Katie," said Franz.

"How's that?" asked Leslie. "Well, you'll learn how to handle a woman as fine as Katie. You won't look like an idiot. That way you can train her to do the things you like. Didn't you learn stuff from, what was her name, Maude? Didn't you learn from her?"

"Boy, I sure did."

"Didn't it make you feel better to know some stuff in front of Rain?" asked Franz.

"Well, yes," said Leslie. "I was not embarrassed with her. And she thinks I'm worldly."

"See what I mean?" said Franz. "You're doing her a favor." The whole time, Daddy Rabbit was laughing his butt off. Leslie went home and hit the rack.

That morning he was up early and took the kids to school and came back to pick up his mom for her rounds. First stop for the day was Suzie Davis's brother Dave Morris's restaurant.

"When did you get their business?" he asked.

"Suzie arranged it for me," she replied. At the restaurant, his mom pointed to the bundles for The Parisian. The laundry was divided into different color bundles, white ones and brown ones.

"Don't tell me, Mom, one color for white people and the other for colored people," he said.

"Yes, son, that's the way it is," she replied.

They took in aprons and towels and tablecloths and linen napkins to the front to Suzie and towels, aprons, and cooks' jackets to the cook staff. The head chef took the laundry and gave them the dirty ones. "Thanks, Mr. Greene," said Brigitta. "Mr. Greene, this is my son, the one in the navy, Leslie Charles. Leslie, this is Mr. John Greene, the head French chef here."

Leslie stuck out his hand and said, "Nice to meet you, Mr. Greene." John Greene did not know what to do. Here was a white man with his hand stuck out and his mother was standing right there. He just stood there for a minute. It was very silent, so silent you could hear everybody's heartbeat. Nobody moved. Everybody was frozen in time. John Greene finally slowly reached out to Leslie's hand. He took it and shook it. He expected Leslie's mother to start screaming, but she just stood there with a mother's smile on her face. "Nice to meet you, Mr. Charles." John thought to himself, *I like this man and his mother. These are progressive people. This is what the world should be.* "Mr. Greene, I had some French food, or at least some kind of Chinese French food, in Shanghai."

John Greene was a colored man from Eagle Street in Asheville. He had joined the army when he was seventeen. He was first a porter then a busboy and then finally a dishwasher in the mess halls in the army. When the Great War broke out on April 1917, John got moved into the kitchen to cook. The army went from 250,000 men to 4 million in two years. John was then sent overseas to Europe to cook. In June 1919, the war to end all wars was over. John liked the way the French had treated him, and he had met a French woman, so he decided to stay in France. Life was good for John and his French wife. They had children and had the life he wanted in America. John cooked in France for fifteen years. The Depression also hit Europe. Most foreign nationals lost their jobs, and this included John Greene. John and his wife had to move in with her parents. They were not fond of John but they took him in. John's children did not look colored. They looked like Arabs or French Arabs. John's wife took sick and died. His in-laws told him to go back to America. They would watch the children and raise them until John could send for them. John came to New York from France in hopes of getting a job. All he could get was day-labor jobs and not many of them. It took John a year of trying to work and walking and hopping freight trains to get to Asheville.

He had a cousin who worked the boiler room at the Langran Hotel. He got John a job as the junior janitor. One evening he was mopping the basement of the hotel when he met Dave Morris, the owner of the French restaurant in the hotel, The Parisian. He told Dave his story. Dave did not believe he was a French-trained chef, but he wanted to see him cook. He took John into the kitchen and asked John to cook French. John made thinly sliced beef with a cream sauce. He then cooked vegetables in wine and butter. He made a chicken dish and another vegetable dish, and he then made a dessert. Dave was very impressed. Although Dave knew nothing about French food, it looked French to him. He gave John the job over three years ago. His business flourished. The Parisian was the best French restaurant in the mountains. Everybody said it was pure French cooking. John told Leslie, "Come in to eat and I'll make something real special for you."

"That sounds great," replied Leslie. Leslie and his mom finished her rounds. Her business was doing very good.

Leslie and Katie had dinner with his family that evening. They had turkey and dressing and all the trimmings. That evening they played cards with his folks. They made plans to go on a picnic tomorrow. It was Saturday and Katie did not have school. Katie had invited Franz and Suzie to go with them. They were going to Mars Hill for the picnic, and Herbert and Stella Charles and Albert and his lady friend from college were going with them. Katie made potato salad, Suzie brought all kinds of French pastries, Stella was bringing Southern fried chicken and two gallons of unsweetened iced tea, Brigitta had Ruth make baked beans and deviled eggs, and Leslie took one of Otto's guitars. They stayed all day in Mars Hill, sitting on the Ivey River at Hattie George's farm. Hattie's family was wealthy tobacco farmers, and they were great friends of the Charleses. They played music and watched and fed the trout in the river. Leslie told everyone of the fish and animals in the marsh around Zigui and of the cranes. Leslie was having one of those "best times in my life" days. Both Franz and Leslie and their ladies really like Albert's new lady. She was a freshman music major and wanted to teach music. She seemed to fit right into the family. Her name was Aubrey Giezentanner, tall and blonde. She played the harp and cello. The trip back was pleasant but long. It was getting chilly outside and very dark. Leslie told Franz to try to make sure they had Katie back before ten thirty and looked like they would just make it. Franz's new car was an Oldsmobile, nice and big and fancy and all black. It had a big straight six in it and would fly. Suzie Davis sat so close to Franz it looked like only one person was in the front seat. Leslie slid over to Katie and starting kissing her. She responded in kind and started trying to get as close to him as possible. The windows in the car started to fog up, and Franz had to roll down the window an inch or two. The cold air woke everybody up, and they really started hugging each other for warmth. Franz took Katie home first, and then he drove to Suzie's brother's home in Biltmore Forest. Since her husband had his fatal accident, she lived with her brother in their parents' home. At the house Franz got out and told Leslie to take the car home because he had to help Suzie with some stuff.

Leslie asked, "Do you need me to stay and help you?"

Franz smacked Leslie on the back of his head and said, "Boy, sometimes I worry about you," and winked at Leslie.

Leslie got the message and left. On the drive home, Leslie thought to himself, *That Franz, he must be the luckiest man on Earth. He's good looking, he's smart, he's rich, he dresses great.* (His mother told him about Franz's passion for nicely fitted men's clothing. As a child living in the woods of Tennessee with no mother, he and his brothers and sister had to wear each other's old clothes. Franz always got Etta's old clothes, dresses, and girls' clothes. The

135

neighborhood children used to tease him and beat him up for it. He had to endure this treatment for almost four years, until Herbert Charles married Stella George. She started making Franz some boy clothes, and eventually the Charleses could afford to buy Franz some young men's clothing. He finally got so mean that none of the other children would mess with him or call him names.) *He's got a new car, and he gets to do it, sex, with a beautiful woman. One of these days, that's going to be me, I hope.*

Sunday morning and the Charles family was up early. They had a great breakfast. On Sunday mornings the Charleses had to fix breakfast for themselves, because Ruth and her sister, Laura Ann, had to go to church. They go at 8:00 a.m., and they don't get out until noon. Mrs. Carter and Mrs. Bagwell usually are the ones who cook the Sunday breakfast. Brigitta just does not cook. The ladies liked to fix pancakes, bacon, sausage, and hash browns. Ruth makes the syrup that goes on the pancakes. She makes grape or apple or pear or cherry or strawberry or gooseberry or, the family favorite, rhubarb/strawberry. The family always had freshly squeezed orange juice on Sunday mornings. Otto was able to have fresh oranges, tomatoes, avocados, grapefruits, and green beans (greasy cut shorts) sent by his railroad buddies in Florida to him. He in turn sent them white liquor (moon shine), really big and fine Christmas trees in December, and quartz crystals from Sweetwater, Tennessee. On Sunday afternoons, Ruth and her sister would always fix a big and heavy Sunday late lunch or early dinner on the Sunday evenings. It was sandwiches or soup. The family would walk down to Montfort Park or walk up to the center of town on Sunday afternoons. This Sunday, Leslie wanted Katie to spend time with him and his folks. She agreed only if Leslie went to church with her. She attended the All Souls Episcopal Church in Biltmore Village. Leslie told her he did not want to go to church, that he thought it was a bunch of junk, that he did not believe in ghosts. Katie started to cry.

Leslie asked, "Why are you crying?"

"I want to go to my church on Sundays, and that's where we will get married and attend as a married couple. That's the church we will raise our children in."

Leslie could tell that this was not the time to argue about it. "Okay, what do I need to do?" he asked.

"Wear a suit and pick me and my mother up at 10:30 a.m. at mother's house, and we'll go to church from there." Leslie put on his black suit with a dark-blue tie. He borrowed Franz's car and picked up Katie and her mother. They drove to Biltmore Village to All Souls. There he met Katie's brother, Bill Scrounce, and his wife, Lucille Scrounce, and their three kids. The family went into the chapel and heard the service. Leslie kept thinking, *How long is this going to last?* The service ended at twelve fifteen, and Leslie thought he was going to get to leave. Katie walked him around the grounds and introduced him to the priest and many of the churchgoers. It took about an hour and Leslie was exhausted. He met a lot of young ladies his and Katie's age. Katie was popular at church, and she knew all the people, so she had to introduce him to everyone. Leslie drove Katie and her mother home. Katie told him that her mother was having Sunday dinner with her brother, so yes, she would eat with his family. Leslie took her to his parents' home. The whole family was there, including his grandparents and all his brothers and sisters and Franz and Suzie Davis. Albert had brought his lady, Aubrey Giezentanner, from Mars Hill College with him. This Sunday for late lunch they had steaks, boiled and buttered potatoes, Swiss chard, grilled onions and mushrooms, pole beans, and homemade rolls. The family made ice cream as a dessert. As usual for this family, at family gatherings or dinners, they would play and sing music. They all gathered and played, and during a song they would change musical instruments with each other; this made the songs fun. Herbert the Horrible would again, to the dismay of his mother, play his armpit or burp a tune. This family had a great time together. Around nine that evening, Katie said good-bye to everyone, and Leslie took her home. Her mom was not home yet from her brother's home. Katie asked if Leslie would like to come in so they could sit on the sofa in the living room. It was too cold to sit outside tonight.

"Sure," said Leslie. Katie put on the radio and got them some tea. They held hands and then started to kiss. Leslie started rubbing Katie's back and shoulders while they kissed. Leslie kept thinking, *How many kisses did he give her?* He slid his hand to her breast and assumed she was going to make him move it, but she did not. He kissed her neck and her shoulders. She laid back on the sofa and let him lay on top of her. He was really getting worked up. He slid his hand under her dress and she let him. Both of their breaths were so fast and hot it was intoxicating. He felt her and rubbed her, and the whole time she kept expressing her love for him. A car drove up and a door closed to a car. Leslie and Katie both sat up and slid away from each other. Leslie grabbed his tea and drained it as Mrs. Scrounce came into the house. Katie got up and asked if Leslie needed some more tea. He said yes as he stood behind her and greeted Mrs. Scrounce. He knew he could not just stand in front of Mrs. Scrounce—she would see what he was thinking about. As Katie took his glass and turned for the kitchen, he turned and sat back down. Mrs. Scrounce just walked by with some food she had brought from her son's home and went into the kitchen to put it away. Mrs. Scrounce asked, "Leslie, when do need to go back to the navy?"

"Tomorrow, ma'am."

"It was nice to see you in our church today. Are you Episcopal?" she asked.

"No, ma'am."

"What is your family's faith, Leslie?" she probed.

"Well, ma'am, we don't exactly have a faith. My dad's family is Jewish and my mother has never said either way," he explained.

"You're Jewish," Mrs. Scrounce exclaimed.

"No, ma'am, I'm not anything."

"Well, just where do you go to church?" she asked.

"Mrs. Scrounce, today was the first time I've been to church since basic training, and I only went in basic training then because it was required."

"You've never been to church? What kind of family is yours not to go to church?" By now Mrs. Scrounce was getting upset, and Leslie wanted out of there. Katie rushed in to the room and walked Leslie to the door.

"Will you come by the school tomorrow before you leave?" Leslie agreed and kissed her good night. He could hear Mrs. Scrounce loudly talking to Katie as he hurried down the sidewalk. As Leslie headed home, he decided to swing by Daddy Rabbit's place but remembered he had Franz's car so he went home. He gave the car keys to Franz. Franz asked if he would like to go to Daddy Rabbit's with him and Suzie tonight.

"Yes, Uncle. I need to talk to you about something in private," replied Leslie.

That night at Daddy Rabbit's, Leslie sat with Franz and Suzie and told them of his evening at Katie's house, not the kissing and almost sex, but of the church and Mrs. Scrounce's part. He told them of the way Katie got him to go to church with her and what she said about when they got married. Suzie talked first. "Leslie, most people go to a church of some kind. Your grandfather and your grandmother work at a church college. Your brother goes to the same church college. It sounds like Katie was brought up in the church, and she wants to stay in that church. You're going to have to decide if you can live that way. You'll lose Katie if you won't go to her church or at least to a church. Can you handle that?"

"I don't know," he answered. "I just don't know."

When Suzie went to the ladies' room, Leslie said to Franz, "I now really miss my white Russian, Rain."

"It's a much easier life with Rain, isn't it, Leslie?" said Franz.

"Yes, sir," said Leslie. "Yes, sir."

When Leslie got home and was in bed, he could smell Katie on his hand. Her scent was intoxicating. Leslie could not sleep, so he went to his parents' sitting area in the garden to think about Katie, to think about church, and to think about Mrs. Scrounce. Leslie is real sure he now does not care for Mrs. Scrounce. Mrs. Scrounce needs to live in China and experience how life is lived there. She would worry more about just getting enough to eat and not worry about whether Leslie goes to church or not. Leslie did not sleep much that night. The excitement of leaving and the thoughts of Katie and the thoughts of Katie's mother kept him awake.

Leslie had an early breakfast with his family. He took the kids to school and stopped at Lee Edwards High School to see Katie. Katie took a break and was excited to see him. She told him she had a gift for him. Leslie smiled and thought to himself, *I think I was just worrying about nothing. Katie is not as worried about religion as her mother.* He opened his going-away gift, and it was a book on the sins of the Jews, a book on how to become a Christian, and a book on how the Episcopal Church was formed. He just smiled to her and said his good-byes.

Leslie went home and packed. He took a lot of pictures with him. He left each of his siblings two dollars apiece. His mom drove him to the train station, and she sat with him and his father until his train got ready to leave. Otto had found him a seat in the caboose on a feldspar train going to Kansas City, Missouri. (Feldspar is a white mineral mined in western North Carolina and used in the manufacturing of nonabrasive cleaners like Bon Ami.) From there he catches a coal train to San Francisco. The trip should take no more than three days. Leslie tried to read his new books that Katie had given him. He tried the first books on the sins of Jews, and after trying to start it a few times, he threw it off the train somewhere in the middle of Tennessee. The next book made it to the Mississippi River before he threw it off the train. He threw the third book off just on the other side of the Mississippi River.

CHAPTER 15

BACK TO CHINA

There were a bunch of new papers from different cities, and that's what he read to kill time. The papers were full of stories of the civil war in China and of the Japanese invasion of China. Some of the papers said it was an Oriental problem, and we had no business involved in it, so we should stay neutral. Other papers said it was Japanese imperialism, and we need to fight them over there instead of letting them come here to fight. The business sections of the paper told of how well our industries were doing supplying European countries in there aggressions. It looked like we were supplying both or all sides. Some papers said it was a European problem and we needed to stay out of it. Other papers wanted us to get involved but were not sure which side we should be for. Leslie was able to reconnect with the same big ship he crossed the Pacific in for the return trip to China by way of Hawaii. Leslie worked hard and trained hard for battle on the cruise. He had a two-day layover in Hawaii, so he called his second cousins at the Royal Hawaiian Hotel gift shop. He ate and talked to Alma and Woodley Patton and stayed at their home for the two-day layover. Leslie thought to himself, *This would be a good life for Rain and me—no, I mean Katie and me, or did I mean Rain? I don't know what I mean anymore. Maybe it's stuff like this that drove Franz crazy, if he's crazy.* Leslie played sorrowful soul music and blues all the way back to China. Leslie could see more sea traffic, and he knew he was almost home, or China. *I call China home.* As soon as Leslie reported back to the *Guam*, he looked up McGhee. He told McGhee all about his adventure home and the problem he thought he may be having with Katie.

Leslie had plenty of work to do now. All the gunboats were taking hits from bullets on every trip upriver. They had lots of holes and dings to fix. As the Japanese got closer to the big cities, more refugees crowded the cities. Every town was in caucus. Food was getting harder to find and getting more expensive. It was two more weeks until the guys had a chance to go to Zigui to see their ladies. This far up the river it was a little more calm and not as crowded. People were going about their daily lives pretty peacefully. The town was now occupied by the Communist army on the left side of the river, and the Japanese were beginning to occupy the right side of the river. It would remain calm until the Japanese had amassed enough soldiers to start crossing the river, and then the fighting would start. The Americans and Europeans were sitting right in the middle of both sides. They were going to remain neutral and protect their governments' interest and the lives of their citizens. Leslie and McGhee headed straight to their little home as soon as they docked. Their part of town seemed quite. The ladies were very glad to see them. Rain spoke a little more Chinese and one or two words of English. Lechou spoke much more English, and she could be understood a little better also. Hojoh was teaching American to Lechou and doing a good job of it.

Lechou was trying to teach Rain. Rain ran up to Leslie and hugged him and squealed, "Reslie, fine to see." Leslie was not sure what she was trying to say but hugged her and kissed her. McGhee got them a cool beer and the couple walked to the garden. Leslie saw a couple of bullet holes in his cranes and his flowers. Lechou made like she had a rifle and was shooting and said, "Communist practice." Leslie decided to move his art work a little further into the marsh to protect his house and Rain and Lechou from stray bullets. McGhee was going to make some repairs to the house, and Leslie and Rain were headed to the market to buy some food. The market was very crowded, but the supply of food was good. Many of the merchants were cooking, and the smells were great. They were cooking every kind of insect, rodent, bird, fish, reptile, and vegetable. The Communist soldiers were everywhere in the markets. They seemed like they were on holiday, except they were armed. Music was being played and children were playing. It was hard to believe this country was in a war against Japan and a civil war at the same time. Every two or three blocks, they were having a chicken fight (cockfight). Civilians and soldiers alike were betting and having a great time. Leslie and Rain turned a corner and were in the middle of an area where men were fighting dogs. Leslie had never seen this kind of dogfighting. Again, men were betting. Everybody seemed to be having a great time. Leslie purchased oranges, mangoes, bok choy, water chestnuts, squash, peanuts, garlic, and a duck. Halfway back to the house, Leslie also bought some rice beers. The market trip took about three hours, and by the time Leslie and Rain returned, McGhee had finished his repairs and was having a beer. Leslie joined him. The boys had a great meal, and each got his bath and gave a bath and made love and went to sleep. Leslie woke up the next day feeling good and refreshed. He then realized he had not thought about Katie at all. That was strange. She had occupied his mind every minute until now. *I wonder what changed,* he thought.

McGhee came into his room and said, "I think I can hear gunfire." They got quiet to listen and it started—the Japanese were shelling the docks. They could hear the screams of the people and the explosions. Leslie told Rain and Lechou to pack. Hojoh came into the house, very excitedly asking, "Boss Leslie, me and my family and you ladies go to America with you now."

Leslie replied, "No no, Hojoh, we're not going to America. We're assigned here in China."

"But boss, the war is here now. We go with you to America."

"Hojoh, America is not in this war. We're neutral. We don't have to leave. We're here protecting American interest, mainly Standard Oil. Nobody is going to attack us," said Leslie.

"Boss, Japanese coming now, they blowing up the docks."

"No. Hojoh, the Japanese are blowing up the Chinese docks. They are not shelling the European or American docks. Hojoh, if the Japanese come, I want you to take the girls and your families to the Communist side. They're much stronger and can protect you," said Leslie.

"I like Communist," replied Hojoh.

"I know," answered Leslie, "and the Communist is strong enough to protect you and your family. Nothing is going to happen today. They're just shelling the docks to scare everyone, start a few fires, mainly just to wreak havoc on the people. Now go home and prepare yourself just in case you really do have to leave," said Leslie.

The Japanese shelled the civilian police barracks and the military police barracks. They blew up the town hall also. They did not fire upon the warehouse district or the manufacturing districts. They wanted all the food stuff and supplies for themselves. The Communist army pulled back to the outskirts of the town and waited for the Japanese to cross the river; they did not. Leslie and McGhee and the ladies stayed at home and watched to see what the Japanese would do. After three days of shelling off and on, it stopped. People started going to see what was left of the docks to see what could be salvaged. The docks and surrounding area were destroyed. Most of the sampans and junks were sunk. There were hundreds of people injured or dead.

Leslie took Lechou and Rain outside and asked, "Is all the money we buried still buried?"

"Yes, boss," answered Lechou.

"Good," said Leslie, "only use that money to stay alive, okay?"

"Okay, Boss Leslie," said Lechou, and she looked at Rain, shaking her head up and down.

Rain looked and then understood and said, "Yes, your love." Leslie knew what she meant. She still could not get some of the words right.

Leslie and McGhee walked down to the docks to see if they could help. They then walked to the European and American areas to see if there were any damages; there was none. The Japanese made sure they did not damage or hurt any Americans or Europeans. Thousands of people were running to the American and European areas. Hundreds of guards were keeping the people behind the fences.

McGhee said, "I wonder where they think we could take them. There are more Japanese on the coast than here, and the Japanese now control a lot of the large metropolitan areas. They needed to go up into the mountains away from civilization."

"Yeah," replied Leslie, "they have a better chance of surviving up in the mountains. We need to get back home to the ladies. The *Guam* will be here tomorrow and we have to be ready to leave."

Rain gave Leslie his bath and they went to bed. Leslie had a great night of lovemaking. Now he considered it lovemaking, not sex. He could not sleep, for he was worried about leaving Rain and Lechou. He did not know when he would be able to get back here, if ever. He worried about his not worrying about Katie. He worried about what people would say about him loving a woman in China. Everybody he knew talked bad about Oriental women. No, wait a minute, Rain is not Oriental. She's white Russian, European. The next thing Leslie knew, it was morning. Rain was up fixing breakfast. She made the eggs, fish, garlic, and finely chopped vegetables wrapped in dough and fried. She put a mustard sauce on then. Rain made enough for everyone and some for Leslie to take back on the ship with him. Leslie and McGhee ate and packed and said there good-byes. The ladies cried and Leslie got very misty-eyed. He and McGhee said good-bye to Hojoh and asked him to keep an eye on the girls and not to let anything happen to them. Leslie gave Hojoh a roll of money and Hojoh thanked him.

The USS *Guam* and four other gunboats, another American, two British, and a French gunboat steamed in. They were escorting two tankers, two cargos, and a passenger ship to Shanghai. These were neutral ships and so were there escorts. The Germans had pulled out of this part of China. They are at war with Great Brittan and France. They have invaded Poland and are now invading Norway. The United States again is neutral and does not want to get into a European war. Economically, the United States was doing well supplying all sides.

It was four months before Leslie and McGhee made another trip up to Zigui. They had spent the past four months at the shipyards in Shanghai repairing and armoring the tankers and cargo ships. Shanghai was a very scary place. Americans and Europeans did not go off base by themselves or by twos. They all went in groups, and everybody in the groups carried there knives. Again, Leslie always carried two. Now McGhee started carrying two knives. When the other sailors would ask why they carried two knives, Leslie would tell them how Daddy Rabbit taught him to fight with a knife\ using two knives. Soon all the sailors on the *Guam* carried two knives. The Americans and the Europeans did not go into Shanghai or the surrounding area after dark either. After dark you could hear gunfire and screams all night long.

"We are not at war with Japan *yet*," their captain would say, "but someday soon. Try to stay away from the Japanese. Don't let them get you into a fight."

The men noticed that the Japanese were cruel and menacing toward the Chinese. They took what they wanted and did not pay for anything.

Leslie received a strange message in one of his letters from home. He got a least one letter and sometimes two from home every week. He received a letter from Katie every week also. The last letter he had gotten from Katie he had not yet opened, and he did not know why. It was only two days old, and he knew he would open it soon. He dreaded it. He was tired of hearing about her church and all of her plans for them when they married. He had good plans also, but she did not seem to want to hear his plans. The letter from home told him his uncle Franz had disappeared a few months back. No one knew where he was. It seems he left in the middle of the night. "Your father was very worried about him at first, but a couple of days after he disappeared, Daddy Rabbit showed up at the rail yard to see your dad. He said Franz had left a package with him to give to your dad and to tell him that he was okay. That he would keep in touch with us through Daddy Rabbit. He left your dad a few thousand dollars. He left Suzie Davis his car and also some money. Son, we don't know why he left or where he went. He rode his motorcycle to Mars Hill to see your grandparents on his way to wherever he went. He left them some money also. Son, your dad is quite concerned," his mother wrote. Everything else with the family was as it was suppose to be. Leslie thought, *Will I ever see Franz again?*

The *Guam* was being reassigned up the river to Zigui, the British reassigned one of its gunboats to Hong Kong, and the Italians pulled their boats out and sent them to the coast of Africa. The Italians had declared war on some of the African countries and needed their ships over there. Some of the men of the Guam had to pack up their Chinese families, and some of the men had to pack up their girlfriends and move them to Zigui. The captain would let these men take their Chinese families and belongings on the ship. The men and their families and girlfriends would move into the vacant homes of the British and Italian families and girlfriends. The British and Italian girlfriends and families that were left behind in Zigui would have to try to meet and become girlfriends of the new American sailors. The Americans had a tugboat towing a barge full of their equipment and vehicles and other belongings to Zigui. The move took about a week.

Leslie and McGhee introduced Hojoh to the officers and chiefs and told them Hojoh could help them find anything they wanted or needed. Leslie and McGhee moved into their house with their ladies. Leslie said to himself, *You know that there is a war going on, and we're right in the middle of it, and I'm living in a country where I don't speak the language, and I'm living with a woman that does not speak English, and it stinks every day, and I think I'm the happiest I could ever be.* McGhee and Leslie had a party and invited three of the sailors from their ship. Lechou had three lady friends attend also. They cooked a sweet-and-sour duck with rice and vegetables with mushrooms and water chestnuts and had cold rice beer. Lechou played the banhu (a bamboo stick on a sounding board with strings, it was played with a bow), Leslie played the pipa (a mandolin-type instrument), and Rain blew the guan (a flute). The party was a great success. The other sailors ate and drank and danced with the Chinese girls. At dusk the sailors walked the young girls home and went to their ship for the evening. Leslie and McGhee sat outside by the garden and drank some beers and daydreamed in silence. What a good life the boys had.

Leslie spent the rest of the spring and summer of 1941 cruising up and down the Yangtze River. The cruise got a little more dangerous on each trip. No one really shot at the sailors or marines, but they did take shots at the crews of the tankers and cargo ships. White people in European clothing were also good targets. Nobody was sure who or what groups were doing the shooting—the Communists, the nationalist, bandits, river pirates, maybe even the Japanese. Every week it seemed like another small village or town was looted and burned.

This war was getting larger daily. The Germans were advising and arming the Japanese, and the Russians were advising and training the Chinese Communists. The Americans were supplying the nationalist army and training its air force and supplying fighter planes. The Americans had also started the Flying Tigers volunteer air force, which was flown by Americans, and it was not real clear which Chinese side they were fighting for. An American aviator ran the Flying Tigers for the nationalist army, and an American marine helped train the Chinese Communist army.

Leslie had decided he would get out of the navy when his hitch was up in December and take Rain to Hawaii to live. He would open a welding shop and also make his lawn art like his cranes and flowers to sell to the tourists. He and Rain could live very much like Woodley and Alma lived. He needed to talk to the XO to see what it would take to take Rain to Hawaii. Now Leslie remembered the last time he wanted to marry someone. She was already married. He would ask Rain this time before he made plans and before he told his parents. Leslie thought of the questions his mother had asked him about Maude that he could not answer. He needs to question Rain about herself. He needed to do this tonight.

Leslie was working at the boat yard in Zigui when McGhee came up to him and said, "Are you ready to go home?"

"Yep, I'm finished. Let's go," answered Leslie.

The boys picked up food and beer at the market on their way home. Leslie told McGhee of his plan with Rain. Leslie met some Russian sailors at the docks this past month and talked to one of their welders every now and again. He decided to take the Russian home with him to help talk to Rain about his plans for them. Rain's English was getting better daily, but she still had trouble putting sentences together. Nakita, the Russian, walked home with Leslie, and the two of them had beers out in the patio by the garden. Nakita told Leslie how nice the house was and how nice the garden was.

Lechou announced that dinner was served. She and Rain prepared chop suey over rice. Leslie asked Nakita to translate his words to Rain for him. Nakita agreed to do it.

"Rain, I want you to marry me and move to Hawaii with me. We could have a home, and we could have children, and we would have a great life together."

The Russian started to translate Leslie's message to her, and then he turned and said to Leslie, "Her name is Irani. It sounds like 'rain' but it's Irani. In American, it means 'Irene.'"

"What is her last name?" Leslie asked.

"Batranch."

Leslie asked, "What is her age?"

"She thinks she is eighteen or twenty, but she's not real sure."

"How did she get here in China?"

149

"Her family fled Russia during the Bolshevik Revolution of 1917. She was born in China about eighteen to twenty years ago to her white Russian family. The Russian village just inside China was invaded by Chinese bandits, and she was put into slavery when she was about twelve to fourteen and later traded to the merchants that sold her to you," said Nakita. "She says yes to your marriage and Hawaii."

Leslie hugged her and said, "We are going to have a great life."

Rain (Irene) said, "I be good husband children with you."

Leslie knew what she was saying and he said, "We're going to have to work on your sentences." That evening, Leslie and Nakita and the girls played their interments. The Russian sailor was very good on Leslie's guitar. They played and sang and drank beers until midnight, and then they turned in and slept well due to exhaustion.

The next four months went by peacefully. Leslie got lots of letters from home wanting him to visit again. He wrote that right now he could not. Katie wanted to know what was going on with him. His letters were vague as to what their future was, and there were less of them. Leslie was now an E5 pay grade and was sending more money home. He told his parents he was getting out of the navy but did not tell them what his plans were after the navy.

Each month different groups of foreign military and their support groups left China. Each shipyard on the river was closing down because of the war. By fall, the American navy and the American marines were ordered to Shanghai. All the men of the *Guam* had to pack up and leave the next day; stuff they could not pack, they were to destroy. Leslie asked the XO what he was to do with Irani. They were getting married and he could not leave her.

"Sailor, you were warned about falling in love with one of these people. You cannot marry a Chinese or take them to the States," said the XO.

"But, sir, she is not Chinese. She is a European," Leslie exclaimed.

"Oh," said the XO, "I did not know that. Where is she from?"

"Russia, sir, she's a white Russian," replied Leslie.

"Sailor, I hate to tell you this, but Russia is on the Asian continent, which makes her an Asian, and the policy says no Asians," said the XO.

"But, sir, she's white and I love her."

"Sorry, Sailor, but the rules are the rules. Say your good-byes and get on the ship in time for it to leave," ordered the XO.

"Aye, aye, sir," said Leslie slowly and angrily. Leslie went home to tell McGhee and Irani of his bad news.

McGhee asked, "What are you going to do? I know you love her and you can't stay here. They won't let you take her with you, so what are you going to do?"

"I don't know. I have to have some time to think," Leslie said as he walked out the back door through the garden and out into the marsh. He reset his art work and walked around. Irani came out to find out what was wrong with him.

"You feel okay with me?" she asked.

"Yes, very much so, yes," he exclaimed. "I love you."

"I love you," she said and got the words right. Leslie thought to himself, *Now is the time I need someone to translate for me.* He walked her into the house and asked everyone to gather around. He wanted to talk to everyone, including Hojoh and his brother. The group gathered and McGhee served beers.

"This is what I want to do. Irani and Lechou stay here, and I want you, Hojoh, and your brother to watch over them until I get back. I'm out of the navy on December 10. I'll try to get out in Shanghai or maybe the Philippines or maybe Hawaii. It does not matter where I get out. I'm coming back here and then Irani will leave with me, and we'll go to Hawaii as husband and wife. I should be back by the new years. That's my plan. What do you think?" Leslie asked.

"Sounds like a plan to me," said McGhee. Hojoh and his brother nodded their heads yes.

And Irani hugged him and said, "I be here for you to get back to."

She got that one pretty close, he thought and hugged her. Irani and Leslie gave each other their baths, and they made love all night long.

Leslie and McGhee had to load up Hojoh's rickshaw with all the stuff they were taking with them and went to the gunboat and steamed away. Leslie was brokenhearted. He had never felt such pain in his chest. He felt like crying all the time. The *Guam* and her men were back in Shanghai and started to set up their base again, when they got orders to pack. The fleet was being resigned to the Philippines. The navy and the Fourth Marines were in that group. Only one marine squad was to stay.

Leslie ask the XO if he could catch an escort destroyer or any other ship going to Hawaii. He was getting out on the December 10 and wanted to get out in Hawaii.

"Why Hawaii?" the XO asked.

"I have cousins in Hawaii, and I think I may want to live there," he answered. "You have family in Hawaii? What do they do in Hawaii?" the XO asked.

"Sir, they own and run the gift shop at the Royal Hawaiian Hotel," Leslie said proudly.

"Let me find out from the old man (a term used for the headman on a ship, the captain)," said the XO. That evening the XO came to Leslie and said, "Let's talk. Sailor, the captain said there is a navy tanker being escorted to Hawaii by a couple of tin cans (escort destroyers). You can catch a ride with them. You'll have to work as part of the crew. Is that okay? The captain wants to know if this has anything to do with your lady friend."

"Yes, sir. I'm going to find a way to bring her to Hawaii when I'm out of the navy. We're going to live in Hawaii," replied Leslie.

"Well, good luck to you, Sailor," said the XO. He shook Leslie's hand and was gone. Leslie went to McGhee and told him of his good luck. McGhee helped Leslie take his belongings to the escort destroyer, and they said their good-byes. They hugged and shook hands. Leslie's new ship left Shanghai the following morning. The seas were a little choppy because it was winter, but Leslie did not get sick. He was proud of himself. He did have to shave, and this ship needed a lot of welding. Leslie felt good on this voyage. He worked hard and played music nightly with different members of the crew. He also made steel cranes for some of his new friends.

CHAPTER 16

HAWAII

They made a good fast trip to Hawaii. He got into Hawaii late Friday night. He called Woodley and Alma and told them he just got into Hawaii. They told him to get a cab and come to their house. It was late and Leslie and the Pattons turned in for the night. At breakfast, Leslie told them of his plans. Woodley asked him if he knew the news from China. Leslie said no. Woodley got Leslie some older newspapers for him to read. The news was very bad. The Japanese had taken Shanghai as well as most of the coast of China. Leslie wired his parents that he was in Hawaii and was with the Pattons and that they should come out to Hawaii for a month. He told them of his plans to stay in Hawaii for a while. That day, Saturday, he and Woodley looked for a shop to set up his welding in and maybe a place to live. That afternoon he took Alma to the base exchange to do some shopping. Leslie decided he was going to cook them an authentic Chinese dinner. He grilled bok choy, and he cooked chicken with rice and vegetables in a spicy sauce. The Pattons loved the food, and Leslie felt proud of himself for not poisoning anyone. The Pattons took Leslie to a floor show at the hotel. It was a variety show with a band. Leslie ask Woodley if he knew anyone in the band.

Woodley said, "Yes, I know all of them. They're local boys. They tour all the military camps on the islands to put on shows. They're famous."

Leslie asked if Woodley could introduce him to them and Woodley said, "Absolutely. After tonight's show I'll give you an intro."

"Great," said Leslie. *I may be able to pick up some cash to play music.* Leslie thought to himself, *Things are looking up for me.*

Sunday morning, December 7, was a beautiful morning. Woodley was going to take Leslie fishing, a kind of fishing that Leslie had never done—stand on the beach in water up to your knees and cast your line out in the surf. Alma was packing them a lunch and was fixing breakfast.

She called to the men, "Breakfast is served for the two fishermen. I hope they can bring back dinner." As the group was laughing, they could hear the sound of many, many airplane engines. All of a sudden they could hear loud explosions. Leslie and the Pattons walked to the street and could see large plumes of smoke coming from the shipyards. Leslie could see Japanese planes everywhere. They were shooting and bombing everything. The group retreated back into their home. Woodley grabbed the phone but it was dead. Alma turned on the radio but it was also dead.

Leslie said, "We need to stay inside until this is over. There is nothing we can do while it's happening." Leslie added, "We need to go into the bedroom and sit on the floor by the bed, just in case."

They sat on the floor for about two hours. They could not hear any more explosions. All they could hear were sirens.

Woodley said, "Let's see if we can help any of the neighbors, and let's try to find the people that work for us. Alma, fill everything that will hold water with water, take stock of what food we have, and Leslie and I will go to the gift shop and see what food we have there."

"Yes, dear. You guys be careful. Should I check the first-aid kit and the medicine chest?" Alma replied. Leslie and Woodley took stock of what supplies they had on hand at the shop. They secured the supplies in the storeroom at the gift shop. Woodley divided the supplies into two—one pile was for the food and supplies that he and his family needed, and the other stack was for donations to the public when it was called for. He and Leslie took a toolbox with nails, a hammer, a wrench, a black tape, screws, and a saw and went out to help their neighbors. Their neighborhood was very lucky. It had very little damage—broken windows, downed power and phone lines, and a few car wrecks. Leslie could look toward the shipyards and see black smoke and fire everywhere. Later that afternoon, Woodley and Leslie went home. Alma had food for them and lots of questions.

"Did you get in touch with the couple that works for us, to see if they were okay?" she asked.

"No, dear, I had no way of contacting them," answered Woodley. At that time the front door opened, and it was the Hawaiian couple who worked at the gift shop for the Pattons.

"Are you guys okay?" they asked.

"Sure," said Woodley. "You guys come on in and join us. Have you heard any news?"

"We heard on the car radio that it was the Japanese and they destroyed Pearl Harbor and the army camp and the army air corps. We are under martial law and ordered not to go out. There are thousands of people dead, mostly military," said the man. "They have also called in all the off-duty military personnel," he also said.

Woodley turned to Leslie and said, "Do you need to report in?"

"I don't know if they mean people like me. I mean I'm getting out in two more days. I'll report in, in the morning. I have to get out so I can go back to China to get Irani," replied Leslie.

The other couple and Leslie stayed with the Pattons that night. First thing that next morning, Leslie put on his whites and reported to the personnel office on the base. He stood in line waiting to get into the building for four hours. When he finally got in he went to the office of the outgoing personnel. The officer asked, "What do you need, Sailor?"

"My tour of duty is finished, and I'm here to get out of the navy, sir," spoke Leslie.

The duty officer turned to Leslie and screamed, "You got to be shitting me, Sailor. Do you know that we were attacked and that we're going to go to war against Japan? What do you mean your time is up? Your time is up when the navy says it's up. Do you hear me, Sailor?"

"Yes, sir, but I have to get out and go back to China to get my future wife," replied Leslie.

"What the hell do you want to marry a gook for?" shouted the duty officer.

"Sir, she's white, and I love her, and I'm sure she's in danger," said Leslie almost in tears.

"Sit down, son, and tell me about it," replied the duty officer. He was now calm and fatherly to Leslie.

Leslie told him all about Irani and their little home and of the Japanese. The duty officer told Leslie that there was nothing he could do and that Irani is probably safer where she's at. That far up the Yangtze—the Japanese could not stretch their forces that far right now. As for getting out, it was not going to happen right now. The navy needed all the men she could get. This was going to be a navy war. The duty officer told him that if he just reenlisted for the war, he would become a petty officer, first class, which was an E6. Leslie asked, "Sir, what are my options?"

"You can reenlist with the hick in pay and rate now, today, right here and now, or you can report tomorrow to try to get out, and you'll be reassigned with no pay raise or rate. It's up to you," said the duty officer.

Leslie said, "Where do I sign up for this war, sir?"

"I'll reenlist you now, Sailor, and personnel will do your paperwork today."

"Thank you, sir," said Leslie. Strange thing was that Leslie felt pretty good about himself. He wanted to go get Irani, but the duty officer may be right. *She probably will be safer nine hundred miles up the Yangtze River. Hojoh is going to look after her, and he should be able to get there within a year.*

Now he has to go to Woodley and Alma's house and tell them what he has done. Back at the house, Alma made him a great dinner. They had frozen fish and frozen vegetables. The freezer was out, and they had no way to store frozen food. They were also going to have to eat two gallons of pineapple ice cream. Woodley and his neighbors grilled a ton of food and told the guests and employees of the hotel to come and eat with them. Over half the guests of the hotel were military families. They also told the local firemen and police to stop in for some food. Neighbors brought pigs' heads, chickens, plenty of fish, and all kinds of fruit. Leslie and some of the men from the hotel band came over, and they played old songs and sang. It was strange that they all had a great time. They ate great food and drank and sang. Some of the women danced the hula. Maybe they had a great time tonight because they knew it would be a long time before anyone was happy again.

Leslie got up and packed only the military stuff he would need to sign back on board. He said good-bye to the Pattons and they to him, and he was off for another adventure in his life. Well, at least he was now a chief petty officer, first class. That meant he got paid more money to do the same job with less people to tell him what to do, and that would be okay too. Everything at the base was in chaos. People were running around trying to find other people, the hospitals were full, the harbor was full of sunken or sinking ships, some of the fires were still burning, and there were shot-up and wrecked vehicles everywhere. Leslie found personnel. There were sailors and civilians asking all kinds of questions with no one to answer them. Leslie started telling everyone to get in line, starting at the door, to form two lines—one for the military and the other for civilians. Everybody started do what Leslie told them to do. It seemed they just wanted someone with authority to start making sense of all of this. Leslie asked the sailors to form two lines, one line for the men whose ships were missing. The other line was for sailors or marines who were just getting to Hawaii and needed to be assigned somewhere. Leslie asked if anyone was a clerk or a typist; about a dozen sailors raised their hands. Leslie instructed,

"You men take down everyone's name, rank, rate, serial number. Civilian employees whose jobs have been bombed, please give your name and occupation and where you worked to this sailor. Are there any firemen or medical staff here? If so please report to the first-aid station closest to where you used to work. Firemen, report to any fire station or fire truck you can see. Policemen or security, please report to the nearest shore patrol or military policeman you see. Three officers came up to Leslie and said, "Can we help?"

Leslie said, "This is my first day here, and I don't know what I'm doing."

A captain said, "You're doing great, Seaman, just great. If it's okay, I'll take over for you."

"Aye, aye, sir," responded Leslie.

"What's your rate, Sailor?" asked the captain.

"I'm a welder, sir. I just made chief, first class," answered Leslie.

"Sailor, gather the rest of these men who are welders, ship maintenance, engine room people, and construction crews and take them to the harbor. There will be plenty of work for everyone. Sailor, put yours and everyone you're taking with you, name on a pad and leave it with me," said the captain.

"Aye, aye, sir," responded Leslie. "Men, if anyone of you work construction, maintenance on a ship, or the engine room, sign here and follow me." Leslie could not believe the destruction and the numbers of ship destroyed and still sinking. He had about forty men with him when he reported to a master chief. The master chief (E9) told each man where to go to work. He told Leslie to start cutting down anything hanging that was dangerous. There were parts of buildings and pieces of ships and airplanes hanging off buildings and vehicles.

Leslie said, "Aye, aye sir," and started to work. Leslie worked until 0300 hours and finally lay down in the back of a truck to sleep.

At 0700 hours, he was awakened by the master chief, "Seaman, get some chow and let's start back to work."

"Aye aye, Master Chief," said Leslie, and he went to one of the outside chow lines the navy had set up. Leslie was still in his dress whites from yesterday, and he had not taken a shower. He looked a mess, but so did everyone else. Leslie thought about home during the day, and he thought about Irani and how she was doing. He also thought about his uncle Franz, who was now a China marine. *How did Uncle Franz get to be a China marine? He was a gangster, and a good one. I'll have to write my dad to find out. I'm sure Asheville was glad to get rid of him.*

THE END OF THIS STORY.
(Look for the story of Franz Charles.)

China Sailor

Please read this part of my book.

My book is about an American family. All the places are
historically correct, and most of the people were real. I
added some people to make a better story. My book is
about a young man growing up in the thirties, how he
lived, how he became a China sailor, how he lived in
China, and how he found his first loves. This is also a
very good love story.

CHARACTERS OF THIS FICTIONAL NOVEL

///

Herbert (pronounced "a bear") Charles—patriarch of the Charles family, born in Switzerland in 1875, brought his family to America in 1906

Stella Carter—married Herbert Charles in 1910

Otto Charles—Herbert's oldest son, born in 1896

John Charles—second son of Herbert, born in 1899

Etta Charles—only daughter of Herbert, born in 1901

Franz Charles—youngest son of Herbert, born in 1904

Brigitta Miesenhammer—married Otto Charles in 1916

Leslie Charles—first son of Otto, born in 1920

Albert Charles—second son of Otto, born in 1924

John Henry Charles—third son of Otto, born in 1926

Frank Charles—fourth son of Otto, born in 1927

Ava Charles—first daughter of Otto, born in 1929

Sonja Charles—second daughter of Otto, born in 1930

Herbert (pronounced "a bear") Charles—last son of Otto, born in 1932

Colonel Marcus Adams—colonel of marines in China

Petus (Petie) Amundos—second lieutenant in China

Colonel Amundos—father of Lt. Amundos

Captain Barious—Marine Captain Franz is aid to this captain

Buddy Bryant—gambler friend of Franz
Ray Davis—Suzie Davis's dead husband
Suzie Davis—lady friend of Franz Charles

Aubrey Giezentanner—college girlfriend of Albert
Charles M. E. Gray—second lieutenant, marines
Mr. and Mrs. Hamilton—minister and wife in Johnson City
Hojoh—rickshaw driver in China
Second Lieutenant Bob Jolly—marine lieutenant
Lechou—Chinese girl
Lieutenant JG MacConnel—XO of USS *Guam*
Dave Morris—Suzie Davis's brother, friend of Franz
Mr. Noble—teacher at Lee Edwards High School
Daddy Rabbit (Isaiah Green)—best friend of Franz, patriarch of the
    Green family, and bar and gambling club owner
Mattie Blue—daughter of the bartender at Daddy Rabbit's club.
    She was the go-between for Suzie and Franz
Ruth—colored maid and cook for the Charles family
Laura Ann—Ruth's sister and laundry maid for Brigitta Charles
Mrs. Bagwell—boarder of the Charles family and elderly schoolteacher
Mr. Carter—boarder and druggist
Mrs. Carter—boarder and wife of Mr. Carter
Steven Bellich—boarder and draftsman
Martin McCracken—JAG officer
Nurse at Anderson Hospital
George Coppersmith—navy teletype operator
Charles David—navy welder
John Greene—colored French chef at The Parisian restaurant.
Maude Kennedy—lady from Great Lakes
Joe McGhee—chief petty officer, welder, Leslie's best friend in
    China
Don Jones—Asheville chief of police
J. D. Moore—navy lieutenant, junior grade

Katie Scrounce—teacher and lady friend of Leslie

Mrs. Scrounce—Katie's mother and a teacher

Billy Smith—petty officer, third class, welder who talked Leslie into joining the navy

Emery Tanner—captain of the USS *Guam*

Alex Taft—JAG officer

Gay Woody—US Navy fireman

Please read this part of my book.

My book is about an American family. All the places are historically correct, and most of the people were real. I added some people to make a better story. My book is about a young man growing up in the thirties, how he lived, how he became a China Sailor and how he lived in China, and how he found his first loves. This is also a very good love story.

Please read this part of my book.

My book is about an American family. All the places are historically correct, and most of the people were real. I added some people to make a better story. My book is about a young man growing up in the thirties, how he lived, how he became a China Sailor and how he lived in China, and how he found his first loves. This is also a very good love story.